Sweet Dreams

LOVE HAPPENS • BOOK FOUR

SUSAN WARNER

Sweet Dreams

One

"I must have lost my mind. This place looks like it's never heard of Starbucks!"

Kelly Thomson got out of the taxi and stepped into a real-life Norman Rockwell town. The streets were cleaner than her last apartment. And there was no noise to speak of. If she considered the three cars at the light noise, then she supposed one could say there was some noise.

She was officially standing in front of the crazy hotel. It said the word "Hotel" on it. The only time you saw that was in a movie where the heroine was about to be killed in a very painful way. How did this happen? Wasn't it just an hour ago Kelly Thomson had been sitting in first class on a plane to Florida? This was supposed to be an assignment to help her find herself. After making money as a corporate trainer for the last twelve years, she still wasn't feeling fulfilled. She'd seen an ad in the paper that mentioned a volunteer opportunity involving setting up a training center for high schoolers for the jobs of tomorrow.

"Miss, here are your bags." Kelly looked at the young man. He must have been about 25, and he was standing in front of her. She was 36 years old, but she had tracked a lot more miles on this body. Realizing he was still standing there, waiting, she asked, "Is there something I'm missing? Some local custom?"

The boy turned red.

"Lord, I haven't blushed since high school! Go ahead and tell me already."

"Miss, you didn't give me a tip," he said in a quiet voice.

"A tip?" Kelly looked at the boy and then nodded. She got back in the taxi and saw it took credit cards, but she didn't see the place to put a tip. She got out of the taxi and faced the driver.

"There's nowhere for me to put the tip on that machine," she said in explanation. The driver's face fell.

"No, Miss, there isn't. We haven't got the new models that do that yet."

Kelly knew her mouth was open. "I don't have cash."

Now it was the driver's turn to have his mouth open. He closed his mouth and told her to wait on the curb.

Kelly watched him go, thinking there was no way he would leave her on the sidewalk in front of the hotel without offering to take her bags in while he went inside. Well, she was very wrong.

"There you are! You must be Kelly Thomson."

Kelly turned around, and what she saw made it clear as to why the world had rural areas in it. He was magnificent. She'd thought this trip would be a sour experience, but now it was looking up. He must have been about six foot two, tall enough that she could dance with him and he could make her feel all petite and girly at her five foot ten. He had dark hair that she could run her fingers through. All of that was topped with broad shoulders for her to hold on to in case of she didn't even know what, but they were there.

"Yes, I am Kelly Thomson. How can I serve—I mean, help you." As he approached, she realized he didn't look as friendly as he did before.

"I've been looking for you at the airport for the last two hours."

Kelly sighed. She understood a person couldn't have it all. "Did you call the airport for my flight number?" she asked patiently.

He seemed to clench his teeth and then closed his eyes before answering her.

"Yes, I did call the airline, and I gave them your flight number. They said it had already landed when I called, so I thought I was late. When I got to the airport, you weren't there. Then I just got a call from the sheriff saying they knew where my stranger was because Davy was reporting a woman trying to beat the fare."

Kelly looked at him and then back at the hotel. "Beating a fare? I've got enough money to buy that hunk of junk he calls a cab."

"You might, Miss, but you don't have it in cash, so you were going to beat me out of my due. Especially since I helped you with all of those bags."

Kelly looked down at the bags.

"You were reporting me for not giving you a tip for two bags?"

The dark haired man decided to step in at that time.

"Now, now, I can see there are some tempers flaring between us. We need to go back to our corners and safe places so we can talk."

"My safe place is in New York. In my condo. Who

says that, anyway? What are you, some sort of guidance counselor?"

"It's funny, you should say that because it happens to be true."

"There's no way!" Kelly replied.

The dark haired man smiled. "It's true, and never have I been happier with my job choice than now."

Kelly wondered if the self-defense classes would work on him. She was sure he was still within the weight range of the play attackers. Then the driver broke her concentration.

"So, Joshua, how do I get my tip?"

Joshua dug into his pocket and gave Davy five dollars. "Here it is. Thanks for bringing her here."

The young man took the money, gave Kelly a nod, and got into his car. It appeared to Kelly he couldn't get away fast enough. When the taxi was gone, and only she and the man named Joshua stood on the street, which was still incredibly barren, Kelly started.

"I think I've had enough of your interruptions for the day. Now, the least you can do is help me into the hotel."

"Interfering? You've been nothing but trouble, and you've been here less than a day. You can't follow instructions to stay at the airport for a pickup."

"I would have, but the heat was a killer, and they didn't have an air conditioner. The taxi did. Besides, I'm not sure you were really at the right plane anyway. I mean, Delta has a lot of different gates and—"

"You weren't supposed to be on a Delta flight. You were booked on a Jetblue!"

"Yes, well, that was obviously a mistake! Jetblue doesn't have first class."

"Who needs first class coming from New York to Florida?"

Kelly was totally confused. "No one needs first class just because they are coming from New York to Florida."

The dark haired man put up his hands in relief. "Finally, some reason."

Kelly continued. "I suppose if you were just coming from Florida to New York, it wouldn't be necessary. However, I fly first class everywhere, so I never have to consider such things."

He just stopped and looked at her. He had stopped for such an extended amount of time that she had to ask, "Are you okay?"

She left her bags and slowly walked towards him. "I think being in the airport with no air conditioning can be very traumatic for you."

She was right next to him, and she could see now the reason he was so still was because he was taking deep breaths as if he were in a yoga class. She patted him on the shoulder, and his eyes flew open.

"Good job. I'm so glad that you are so in touch with your feminity that you can indulge in such things." With that, Kelly left him standing there to put her own bags in the hotel.

This day couldn't be happening. Joshua Case knew this was a bad idea from the very start. He'd told them that this was going to be a bad idea, yet no one had listened to him. Why would they? He was just the guidance counselor. He was the one who knew how things worked. Most importantly, he was the one who would be here long after the experiment was done.

When Cade Designs was being built, they decided that they would also start a vocational program for the kids here. When he had been approached, he'd thought it was a great idea. Lydia Mason, soon to be Lydia Young, had decided to call on him because they both ran a young men's outreach. What he didn't count on was Ethan and Adam Cade calling in a trainer. He had been guiding the students of Castle High School on what to do and how to discover new ways to land their chosen career. But it seemed that while he could guide them to a career, he wasn't the one to train them.

Offering some last minute input, he asked if they could propose the position as a volunteer position. Joshua thought if he put it up as a volunteer position, then they would find someone who was committed to the craft of training.

Two weeks later, Adam Cade sent in a picture of one of the most beautiful women he had ever seen, and she was supposed to be the trainer. If they hired this woman, they'd have all the guys applying to the class, but no one would be learning.

When he asked them what they thought about her qualifications, a lot of chuckles filled the room. At first, he thought that meant they were joking about hiring her. Then, when the laughter died out, Ethan held up his hand to quiet everyone and passed out a paper.

It was her resume. She was one of the most wanted trainers on the East Coast. After he read that, and then looked around the room, that was when he knew that it didn't matter if he agreed or not; he was about to get Kelly Thomson as his new trainer.

He had resigned himself to that fact. At least he thought he had resigned himself to that fact until today. Her photos didn't do her justice. She had auburn hair that danced around her shoulders. She had on pants and a top that hugged a slim frame whenever an errant breeze came through. Joshua thought there must be some mistake; this woman wouldn't do anything for free. Just her statement alone that she didn't fly anything unless it was first class was enough for him to know she was the wrong one.

Her? Around kids? That was just never going to happen. She had the sensitivity of a rhino. She couldn't even tell the difference between him trying to find the strength to keep his voice at an appropriate level when dealing with a woman and her misconstruing it with him getting in touch with his feminine side. He was sure all of his sides were balanced.

It didn't matter. He had to put all of this behind him. What really mattered is what would work for the kids. The sooner he got her out of here, the sooner they could find someone who could really help.

Joshua went into the lobby of the hotel. He could see the clerk getting flustered. When the clerk saw him, he was relieved, and he could see the young man pointing at him. When Kelly turned around, she had a frown on her face. The frown did nothing to detract from the woman's beauty. When she saw it was him, he could see the moment of sympathy flutter across her face before she started her walk to him.

"You know, with all of the back and forth out there, I'm afraid we have not had the opportunity to have a proper introduction. I'm Kelly Thomson, I can train anything, and I'm at your service."

Joshua was speechless. It must have shown because she laughed at his response.

"Don't worry. I'm not just another pretty face, and I can make that statement because I can back it up! Now, do you think you can find your tongue and talk to me, or is it going to be like this the whole time I'm here?"

When Joshua finally did get his speech back, he said the first thing that came to him.

"You do know there isn't any payment for this."

Kelly gave him a smirk and put her hands on her hips.

"Do I look like I need money?"

"Unbelievable."

Kelly laughed. "I have that effect on people. Now, your name?"

"Joshua Case. My name is Joshua Case, and I'm the school guidance counselor at Castle High."

"Ah, you're the rookie that's riding shotgun while I set this up."

Joshua just let it go. "I guess we'll find out."

Kelly gave him a smile that would have given anyone pause. "Now I'm sure you wanted me to know your name and your function. Which I appreciate very much, but was there anything else you wanted to tell me?"

Joshua was looking at how her lips were perfect. They were a perfect bow. When they stopped moving, and his brain caught up, he shook his head and replied, "Yes. We thought it would be too inconvenient for you to be in the hotel. We have a cottage for you to stay in. I'll drive you over."

"That would be great. My bags are at the front desk. Once you get those, we can be on our way."

Kelly didn't need a lot of time. She looked over the cottage and made some notes in her notebook. She made sure she had her flash drive and a laptop just in case. The trip to the community center was short, and when she arrived, there were two men there. One of them she knew—Joshua Case—and the other one was someone she'd only seen via Facetime—Ethan Young. When she walked in, Ethan turned to greet her.

"Hello, Ms. Thomson."

"No, please call me Kelly. I'm so happy to be here today." She looked over at Joshua, who looked as if he had just swallowed a lemon.

"Please, Kelly, feel free to call me Ethan. If you said Mr. Young, I'd think you were talking about my father."

"Joshua," she said with a nod. She didn't wait for his response. Kelly always kept herself focused, and the focus was the client, Mr. Young. He had offered her his first name, but if this presentation didn't go the way he wanted it, they'd be back on last name basis.

Kelly had tons of clothes, but she must have spent the better part of a day picking every outfit she had brought along. Today she was wearing a red and white top with black pants and mini heels. The whole effect was supposed to give off a friendly, feminine, and knowledgeable vibe. She had passed that hurdle because she saw no worried glances between the men.

This presentation was a beast for her to make. Normally, she knew exactly what her clients wanted. She knew what they wanted to accomplish. When she had been interviewed by Ethan, had given one of the most honest replies she had ever received.

"We're new. We have funding money, but we don't know what we should be presenting to our children in our high schools. We care about our children, but we don't know how to get them beyond our sights."

The message was bold, and when she heard it, she was sure that she had made the right decision to take this assignment. She'd worked hours on put-ting together a simple but elegant presentation. The presentation was a walk through what was already known to what could be.

Now that she was here and about to present, the butterflies started; it was as if it were her first presentation. Kelly put on her best smile and started the presentation. This is what she did. She learned new things, and then she taught them. Now it was time to earn her keep for someone else.

"We all want our children to be prepared for the future. But we fight over where they should go and how they should do it. Depending on when you were born, you were raised thinking there was a safe occupation that your child could go into. It used to be doctors and lawyers. Today you'll hear more people talking about computers and security. The vision I have for the training center is this: we first teach problem-solving and creativity and then show them how to take that into their chosen fields. Children are unique and adaptable. We shouldn't try and catch the new wave; we should show them how to manage and excel in a field that interests them."

She followed it up with several other graphs, building layouts, and projection costs. By the time she was finished, she had to excuse herself for a moment to get water. When she came back, the room was all smiles.

"That was exactly what we were looking for," Ethan said. "This is a near and dear project to my fiancee's heart. I know she will be very pleased when I show her the presentation and the plan. What do you think, Joshua?"

Joshua nodded. "I have to admit I was impressed. I really liked the approach and the way you've taken into account the uniqueness of each child. It didn't feel like a cookie cutter solution. I have to ask, who helped you with the presentation?"

Ethan's eyebrow raised as he heard the question. Kelly caught Ethan's movement and placed a hand on his forearm.

"Please, Ethan, don't look poorly on Joshua. I have to say that I have more than once been prejudged by others. I spend a lot of time working on how I look so I can't get upset when it sends off the wrong signals."

She turned to Joshua. "As for your question, no one helped me. I do happen to have a Bachelors in Business, a Master's in Education, and I'm working on my Ph.D. in psychology. I try to keep ahead of the curve when it comes to my career."

Joshua bowed his head. "I stand corrected."

"Really, it's no bother."

Just when it looked like Joshua might have said something else, Ethan jumped in.

"Just so the both of you know, I will be going back to New York. Lydia has decided to run a large fundraiser to get more money for this project. She wants it to be a pilot for other places. If you have any questions, please feel free to reach out to my assistant, Penny."

Ethan patted Joshua on the back and then shook

Kelly's hand.

"I'll leave you two to it, then."

When he left the room, Joshua waited for her to gather her items and then offered to drive her to her place.

"Are you ready, Kelly?"

She picked up her head and nodded.

"Always."

Two

"Could you come in?" Kelly asked.

Joshua knew this wasn't going to work out. But he wasn't a runner. He wasn't sure what to expect from Kelly Thomson, but whatever it was, he was sure it would be the exact opposite of what he thought. When they were both in her cottage, she led him through the house and out to the backyard where there was a porch. She offered him one of the two seats on the deck, and he waited.

"Joshua, it seems we have a problem."

He gave her a small smile. If nothing else, he would say she had a gift for understatement. Here they both were sitting on the porch during the best part of the day. It was just cool enough to be out, and if the news could be believed, it was going to be a scorcher. He looked up at the blue sky and then took a breath, settling down to hear whatever Kelly was going to propose. He was fortunate, and he could listen to her. After that presentation and hearing her credentials, he had to admit he had jumped to conclusions based on her looks.

"It appears, Joshua, that we have to work with one

another, but we haven't started out on the right foot. What can I do to address this?"

She sounded so reasonable that Joshua had to give it a try. Although what he really wanted to say was, 'I'd like you to leave your great idea and be on your way so I can take care of my kids.'

"I know you've somewhat addressed this, but I have some concerns when it comes to working with the kids. Maybe if you could explain to me what you think your role is in this project, then I would have a better understanding."

Kelly's smile turned into a grin. The sardonic raise of her eyebrow was indicative of the answer he was about to receive.

"I realize that I'm not a mother and that I don't have any nieces or nephews, but I think I know how to act around kids."

He found himself looking at her mouth again. It was in the same bow shape that it was before. He wondered if she had gotten it specially fixed like he had read in a magazine so that it stayed that way. He imagined that it must be interesting to live a life when one is obviously beautiful. Joshua thought about the program and how more than fifty percent of the program was made up of young males. Then, all of a sudden, the haze fell away.

If he was having a problem keeping himself on track, how did she think she was going to keep a class of hormonal young males on track to learn anything? He wanted to get the training center, and he had said he would be open, but he wasn't sure this was the way to go.

"I take it from your delayed answer that you are skeptical that I know how to handle myself around children. Let me assure you that I've been at several schools before."

"It's true; I read your resume. Sweet Blooms is a little different is all I'm suggesting."

Kelly sat back in her chair and took a breath. Then she popped up.

"Forgive me." She left the porch and came back in a flash. When she sat down, she handed him a bottle of water. He almost smiled at her consideration. It wasn't lemonade or tea, but it was a beverage, and he had to give her credit for that.

He popped open the bottle and chugged a third of it down. After a few moments passed, she broke the silence.

"So, you're not going to make any comments at all?"

"I'm thinking."

"Ahh."

"Well, my mother always told me to look at the good first, so let's start there. I think you are a very honest person. That's important if you want to work with kids."

"I try to be. Let's not belabor that point, because I'm human like everyone else. However, when I can, I try to be forthright. Like yesterday when you made a mess of things."

Joshua sat up and looked at her laying back in the chair.

"I stopped you from going to jail."

"After thinking about it, I realized it could have all been fixed if you would have double checked your details and not waited until the last minute to do so. I assure you my flight was booked three days before I arrived. A simple phone call would have avoided all of that unpleasantness."

Joshua laughed. "Well, you're welcome."

Kelly took a sip of water and gave him a half-hearted sigh.

"Tell me, Joshua, how long have you been a guidance counselor?"

"It's been about twenty years. I'm forty, and I started in the field at twenty. We found funding for my position full time about twelve years ago."

"I want you to know I respect your experience, and I think we will be able to work with each other if we remember that we're here for the children."

"Is that why you're here, for the children," Joshua asked.

"Yes, contrary to what you see, I started out in a different place from where I'm sitting today. I think all children deserve an opportunity."

Joshua smiled. "The guys will love to hear that from you."

Kelly looked at Joshua again. "I feel like there was a double entendre there."

"Let me be as candid as you are. Why does a woman who looks like you become a trainer?"

"As opposed to what, a model?"

Joshua shrugged. "I guess."

"Because beauty fades and it's fickle. What's beautiful today is ugly tomorrow. I made a decision that my looks would be second, and my brain would be first."

"I admire your spirit, and I think you are a nice person."

"How big of you. I'm sure I hear a *but* coming along."

"But being in Sweet Blooms is a big adjustment from being in the city."

"I knew that before I came."

"The taxi didn't think so, but even beyond that, a woman as beautiful as you is used to a certain kind of living and being treated a certain way, and I'm just not certain you'd be able to adjust to our traditional lifestyle."

"I happen to like things and people from all over, and it's part of my job to be flexible to every environment that I go to."

Joshua heard the words coming out of her mouth, and she sounded like she would be perfect, but he didn't see how she could reconcile the second and third looks she would be getting. She would be a distraction.

He stood up and finished drinking the rest of the water.

"Well, that about sums up everything I can say on the issue," he said. "I'm going to be heading to the school."

Kelly walked him to the door.

"Joshua?"

He was already down the steps when she called, and he turned around.

"I think it would help me if I went to the school to meet the kids before we actually started doing anything. It will help me with the curriculum and to customize my ideas."

She was a vision. The wind ruffled her hair, and the sun hit her at just the right angle. She couldn't have planned a more perfect shot. Joshua shook his head because he knew she was totally clueless. She had been born beautiful. It was hard for him to believe that she wouldn't have gotten special treatment because she was beautiful.

"I think we should just stick to your plan," he said.

"The kids are a bit raw and can be rough. You know, with hormones and drama happening to them every five minutes."

Her hands went over her chest, and she leaned against the door jamb.

"If I didn't know any better, I'd think you were saying I can't handle being around a bunch of high school kids. I was a kid once, you know."

Joshua took the stand. "I'm thinking you're a woman, and the boys are boys, and you can't help who you are."

Kelly nodded. "I'm not the right kind of woman to be around your kids, is that it?"

"I'm saying what I think would be best for both parties."

Joshua knew he sounded wrong, but he had to think about the kids. This woman would waltz in with a whole bunch of young men who barely kept it together on their best day, and it would be a fall out fest on who could impress her first. They would be trying to top each other and get her attention, and the only way they would be sure to get her attention would be to get into trouble. No, he wouldn't risk his kids.

He could tell he had offended her when she stood up and her face tightened up.

"Well, good day to you, Joshua Case."

Castle High had once been a factory filled with a bunch of seamstresses. The space had been cheap when it was in use, and later on when the owners abandoned it, and the property was given to the county, the building had been repurposed to be a school. It was already broken up into classrooms. Joshua had worked in other schools, but due to its history, this high school had a different feel to it. It was roomier and had larger classrooms and wide hallways. His office was on the first floor, as were all of the administrative offices.

Today he was doing his walkthrough to make sure the children who had trouble getting to class saw him. The ones who were on his watch list, he wanted to see them in their classes, and for them to see him at the door looking in on them. If any of his kids were missing or in distress, he would be there. It gave him the opportunity to see them with his own eyes, and if they wanted to see him, they could get up and come to the door on the pretense he had called them. That was the protocol with all of his kids.

He would rather they get up and say they need a break, leaving him to deal with the teachers than to be too late to help a child. He knew all too well what it was like to arrive too late.

School opened at seven thirty to allow kids to come in for breakfast. The first class started at around eight thirty. He didn't do his rounds until nine. It was more than enough time for everyone to get into their classrooms. It was a quiet time for Joshua to walk through the halls.

It was the time that he could take to think about all of the things that were on his mind, and today, there was only one person on his mind. He kept going over what had happened yesterday. Joshua knew he had been wrong. He also knew why. No matter how he looked at it, he was going to have to face the truth that he had been out of line the other day towards Kelly. There was no good answer for it. The only reason he could come up with was that he was infatuated with Kelly. He let his own shortcomings get in the way of what was best for the kids. But more importantly, he had judged her unfairly based on nothing other than what he saw.

Joshua knew better than to judge people. After all, he was the surviving twin. He was the one that people would talk about when he wasn't looking. He was the one that everyone watched to make sure that what had happened once wouldn't happen again.

As he was walking down the hall towards the math class, he heard a familiar voice. It was the voice of the person who was currently on his mind. The gentle tones of her voice carried outside the classroom and drew him like a siren. He peeked inside the classroom, looking through the rectangular window at the door, and sure enough, there she was. She was standing in front of the class talking. He couldn't make out exactly what she was talking about, but what he could see was that every child in the classroom was completely enthralled with her. All of the fears that he had harbored yesterday were all unfounded, and today she had proved it.

Gone was the corporate executive of yesterday. Today, standing in front of the classroom was a woman who could have been a resident of Sweet Blooms. Her hair was tied up into a ponytail, and she had on blue jeans and a cream colored top; all of it said she was a local.

Standing in front of the classroom, gone was the model he had seen yesterday; what he saw today was a woman could work a room no matter who was in it. She went up and down the aisles, and even he leaned a little closer, hoping to hear what was being said. Then, just when he thought he should open the door to hear what was going on inside, all of the children jumped up and cheered.

He saw Kelly go back to the front of the class. Then she turned to the teacher and gave her a hug. After that, she waved to the class as if she were a departing princess, and all of the class waved back. When she put her hand on the door and opened it, she saw he was standing there, and the expression she had went from joy to defensiveness in a heartbeat.

He knew what he had to do, but knowing what you had to do and doing it were two different things. He held the door open, and Kelly stepped out. Their gazes met, but he didn't look away.

"I was wrong," he said to her.

"Yes, you were," she agreed.

She didn't break eye contact with him. Her eyes were brown orbs that looked like the richest sable, and right now, they held no friendly welcome in their depths.

"You're not going to make this easy, are you?" he muttered. "I know better than to judge a book by its cover, but I have to tell you I was really taken in by your cover."

"Was that supposed to be an apology? I was out of line because you were born the way you were?"

Joshua clenched his jaw. "I'm making this worse, but I'm trying to do the right thing."

"You know what you need is some practice coming off that high horse you live on. I came here to help the kids, not to give you free therapy services."

"Enough. I was wrong. I'm asking you to move past

my bad judgment," he said with a huge sigh. "Let me try to make it up to you," he added. "Why don't I introduce you to one of the students who will be enrolling in the program as soon as we have it up? He's a sophomore."

"Are you sure?" she asked.

"Yes, I'm trying, Kelly."

"I'm glad I finally pass muster."

He knew this wasn't over and that he was starting in the hole, but he at least she was open to talking to him.

"I just want to say that the kids can be a pain in general, which has nothing to do with you."

"Does that mean you are going to run interference for me? That you'll help me out to make up for your presumptuousness?"

Joshua smiled. "Well, if I hadn't just seen you in the classroom, and if we hadn't just had a conversation about how high-handed I was, I might have, but now I've learned, and I now know you don't need any help at all."

Kelly smiled at him and gave him a nod. "Just making sure we've really learned."

"I'm not known for giving anyone a break."

"Don't worry, neither am I."

"When is a good time for you to meet the student?"

"Let me know when you two normally meet, and I'll meet you there."

With that said, she turned and went down the hall. As she walked down the hall, Joshua couldn't help but watch her go. Yes, he had made a mistake. Watching her walk away, he realized there was a lot more to Kelly Thompson than what he originally thought. If everything worked out the way it was supposed to, he was going to be with this woman for the next couple of weeks, day in and day out.

Well, that meant the awkward part had already passed. He had already told her he was attracted to her, period. Now the only thing he had to do was make sure he could keep his focus.

Today was the meet and greet. It was the first time that Kelly had ever done a meet and greet with someone who wasn't paying. This was also the first time she had ever done a job that she wasn't getting paid for either. Today's meeting had been set up by Joshua. He had invited some of the kids that he thought would be interested in the program. She was hoping that by talking to everyone today, she would be able to work out any problems before the training began.

Joshua had told her he had picked the kids who had shown the most initiative and the most interest. Still, Kelly wanted to make sure that she had an airtight presentation. This was the opportunity she had been waiting for. She could tell this was the thing she had been waiting for in her career. Once again, she felt that thrill right before she was about to speak to the crowd. That feeling had been gone for so many years.

For the last five years, she had just been going into training after training with no satisfaction at the end, and no feeling that it was making a difference. It was just routine after routine. But today she was getting ready to talk in front of a bunch of high school students. And in doing something for free, she was rediscovering the joy of doing something she loved and was really good at.

She was once again back at Castle High School. Joshua had given her the directions to the classroom where she would be presenting. At first, she thought she was going to have to go and use a projector. Now she was glad she had decided to give handouts. She walked in, and everybody was already there. One girl and two boys, with Josh sitting in the back.

Joshua was something else she would have to look into later on. He had taken her totally by surprise when he had apologized. She remembered seeing him trying to figure out how to apologize. Kelly thought it said a lot about Joshua's character that he was willing to apologize even when he wasn't really clear on how to go about it. She could recognize that she and Joshua had a lot in common. It was true they obviously looked nothing alike. And they didn't even work in the same kind of environment. But what was clear was that both of them were committed to their course of action.

Joshua stood up in the back of the room, and all of the attendees turned towards him.

" Hey guys, today you were called here so you could meet with Kelley Thompson. Kelly is going to be the person who sets up and designs our new training center. Kelly thought it would be a good idea if all of you could meet, and you could ask her any question that you wanted."

As if all of them were connected, they all turned at the same time and looked at Kelly.

"Hello everyone," Kelly said as she stood up in front of the room." I want to thank you all for inviting me here today, and I want to hear what all of you have to say. Ask me any questions that you can come up with."

The first person to speak was an older boy with brown curly hair. He must have been at least six feet tall and was as skinny as a lamp post.

"The first thing I want to know is, do all trainers look like you?"

Both of the boys in the room started to giggle. The other student was a girl, and she just rolled her eyes. Joshua got ready to stand up, but Kelly put her hand out to stop him, and she looked at the boy called Davy.

" I don't know what all trainers look like, but asking me that is a lot like me asking you if all the sophomores in Sweet Blooms look like you."

The second boy in the room—his name was Paul, according to Joshua—started to laugh right away.

"None of us looks like Davy. If we were all like him, we'd starve because he couldn't move his own oxen even if they were sleeping." Sally laughed, and Joshua settled down in the class.

"You were all given a copy of the plans. You can ask me about the plans, or you can ask whatever you want."

After Kelly had extended the invitation, she could see that Joshua looked a little nervous in the back. He started to fidget in his seat, and she wondered what the problem was. Maybe he was just having second thoughts. Whatever it was, she was determined to not focus on him but on the kids.

"Are they paying you to do this?" Sally asked.

"No, they're not. In fact, they're not giving me any money at all," replied Kelly.

"Then why are you doing this?" asked Davy.

"The answer to that question is really complicated, but the simple answer is I'm doing this because I believe in it. I'm doing this because once upon a time, somebody did it for me."

Paul shook his head. "I have to tell you that a lot of people come to our school, and they talk a lot about trying to help us. All of them say that they know what's going to be the best thing for us. Why do you think you're going to be any different?"

Kids, thought Kelly. Kids knew how to get to the heart of every issue. It was probably one of the reasons she hadn't become a teacher. But she was here now, and he had asked the question, and she had said she would answer any and all questions. She looked to the back of the room. She could see that Joshua seemed a little worried. Then she turned to Paul and answered his question.

"I think I might be a little different than the other people who have come to your school, Paul. I know it doesn't look like it, but I was once a foster kid. When I was in one of my many foster homes, there was a woman who took the time to tutor me."

Sally chimed in. "You are a trainer. You must have been really smart, even from the very beginning."

Kelly shook her head.

"I know it must seem like that, but I have to tell you I went to third grade twice. I was so embarrassed because I was the tallest girl in my class, and everybody knew."

Davy looked a little skeptical.

"Nobody can do a grade twice!"

"When I was a kid, you could do a grade twice, and sometimes you could do it three times!"

Sally nodded her head in agreement.

"I heard my mother say that there had been a time when people would have to redo a grade, but she told me that was a long time ago."

Ahh, yes, thought Kelly. The other reason she didn't teach kids was because they always had a way of reminding a person just how old they really were. It was at that moment that Joshua stood up.

"Do you have any other questions for Kelly?"

Sally and Paul shook their head, but Davy turned towards Joshua and then looked back at Kelly. He began to wiggle his eyebrows. "Mr. C, you called her Kelly?"

The room broke out into howls, but Joshua ignored them all. He walked over to stand in front of Kelly and thanked her.

When the door closed, she could still hear them joking with him over the use of her name, but she felt good. She felt so good she wanted to run to Aldo's and buy some shoes, but she was sure there wasn't an Aldo's shoe store in town. She'd have to find her other reward. She knew it would be here. She couldn't think of any place that considered itself civilized that didn't have chocolate.

Three

Kelly had gotten the good news this morning. Everyone was happy with her plans, and the children were excited about what was coming. Upon hearing it, one would think that she would be thrilled, but she understood there was still one more thing that had to be addressed. It was time to introduce Joshua to the rules.

Kelly had already made her money, she'd already gotten in education, and she didn't need to work ever again if that was what she chose to do. Coming to Sweet Blooms was her hail mary pass at trying to find some purpose in her life. In a few short days, she had discovered there was something else that she wanted to do with her life. Kelly had discovered she wanted to do volunteer work. Just because it was volunteer work didn't mean there were no rules.

Kelly thought about the way she had met Joshua. Keeping their first meeting in mind, she knew she needed to have this talk. Ten minutes later she was pulling into Castle High's parking lot. It was about four o'clock. She knew Joshua would be coming out at any time. As if on cue, he walked out of the school.

She got out of her car and stood in front of it so he could see her. Today she had on her corporate wear. She knew he'd be able to spot the red scarf around her neck.

He walked over with a man behind him. The man leaned over towards Joshua, and both of them approached her.

"You must be Kelly Thomson, the trainer," the man said, holding her hand with both of his. When she pulled hers back, he had a sheepish look on his face. Then he continued.

"I'm Dorian Potts, the school principal. I wanted to thank you for helping us out."

"Truly, it's a pleasure," Kelly replied.

Dorian was in his mid to late thirties. He had a few extra pounds on him but nothing that made him stand out. In fact, if Kelly had to describe Dorian, she would have said he was the type of guy who would be totally overlooked. He wasn't tall. They were eye level, and she was in flats, so that put him around five ten.

"I know you're here for the initial contract. Do you have any plans on staying after that? To stick around?" Dorian asked.

"I'm not clear on what my plans are right now. I do know I'll be here long enough to see this project up and running."

"Oh, good. That's good. Maybe I'll see you around. I know a woman like you can be very busy, and our town doesn't offer a lot of activity," he said apologetically.

"It's no problem. I have always found a way to keep myself entertained," Kelly replied.

"Maybe if you're here long enough, you might want to look into doing some teacher training?

We don't really have funds for that kind of thing, but it would be good if we could try and be more up to date," he said.

"Schools are big in the news. Have you tried to petition for more money?"

Dorian shook his head. "It's so competitive, you know. We try, but we're not that big in the grand scheme of things. That's why, if you had time, it would be great if you could help us out. I mean, after the children are done, of course."

"Of course."

"Yes, well, I'll be on my way. Joshua, thank you."

When Dorian walked away, Kelly gave him her best fake smile.

"Oh, yes. Thank you, Joshua."

Joshua took a breath and shook his head.

"To be fair, I didn't know you were going to come by after work."

Kelly nodded. "Uh, huh."

"I'm sure you didn't come by to talk about the principal," he said.

"In an odd way, I did come by to do just that. I wasn't sure if he wanted to ask me out or if he wanted to get me to volunteer to train the teachers for free."

Joshua shook his head. "I agree, it was bad."

"I think it's more important if we talk about rules."

"Rules?"

"Yes, rules. You know, those funny things that people have to follow so that we can only work well together."

"This shouldn't take long because I only have two rules."

"Okay, I'm listening."

Kelly counted them off on her fingers.

"Rule number one: everything I make in terms of the material has to have my name on it as either the creator or contributor."

Joshua shrugged.

"I'm okay with that."

"Good, and the second rule is, I don't have or engage in personal relationships with clients."

Joshua stopped in his tracks.

"I thought we were past that."

"We are. I'm just telling you as a matter of basic principle."

Joshua laughed. "I want you to know I have gotten over my issues with your appearance. I don't deny you are a handsome woman, but I'm only interested in you being able to do your job."

"Good," she said with a smile.

"Good," he echoed.

"Well, then, my work is done, and we can meet up tomorrow and get started."

Joshua agreed. As Kelly drove off, she looked in her rearview mirror and saw Joshua hitting his hand against his forehead.

"I hope you work it out, Joshua. For all our sakes."

The next day Joshua decided to take Kelly to Banter House, the neighborhood diner. He hoped there was something at the diner that she could eat. Every time he thought he knew what she was going to do, she did the opposite. Today wasn't going to be any different.

This morning, he'd asked Kelly if she could meet him for lunch. She said sure. He thought she would show up in jeans after he told her it was going to be at a diner. He was so wrong.

First, she was on time. Second, when she arrived, she stood at the front of the diner dressed in a blue jean dress. He was going to have to face it—Kelly looked good in everything. He gave himself a once over to make sure there were no stains on his clothes. As she made her way to the table, heads discreetly turned to follow her to see who she was meeting with. By the time this lunch was over, he was sure the rumor mill would have them with two love children and on their way to the pulpit.

When the waitress came over to give them their menus, she dropped the menu in front of Kelly. The young lady gave him a smile, and she gave another disgusted glance at Kelly before she walked away. He couldn't see that Kelly had done anything wrong, but still the waitress was borderline rude to her. The only saving grace was that Kelly hadn't looked up from the menu to bear witness to the behavior.

After the waitress left, two waiters came over to the table; both of them had two glasses of water. Each one tried to get Kelly's attention, but she never even looked up. After both of the waiters had left the table, Kelly spoke.

"I thought it would be different in a small town," she said with sadness in her voice.

Joshua was still looking at the waiter, trying to decide who would bring out the food.

"Are we talking about the food?" he asked.

She looked up, confused.

"Oh no, I wasn't talking about the food. Is there a problem?" she asked. "I was actually talking about the meeting with the principal."

"Did you even see the scene that happened with the two waiters?"

"Waiters?" She looked around as if she were looking for them.

"The two waiters who came over to give you water. They looked like they were going to finish the discussion of who could serve you in the back alley."

He could tell from her expression that she had no idea what he was talking about.

"I'm sorry. I didn't see anything but the menu. I didn't eat breakfast, and I'm starving."

"They were rushing to serve you."

Kelly waved it off.

Joshua stared at Kelly as she viewed the menu. He could tell she wasn't affected by anything that was going on around her. He couldn't imagine what it must be like to constantly have people falling over themselves around you.

"I guess Helen of Troy eventually got used to it as well," he said. After that, he followed her lead and looked over the menu. He didn't have to, though; he already knew he was here for a bacon burger.

"What did you say about Helen?"

"Nothing, I was just reminiscing. Have you decided what you want?"

She looked up, and her whole face was transformed by her smile. She looked like a kid about to get into trouble.

"The town is just filling up with attractive people. I don't know if they expect people to come to Sweet

Blooms because we have all the old shops or because we're collecting all the attractive people. I'm Geeta. I'm out here because I have two waiters who wanted to fight it out in the back over which one of them would get to marry you."

Geeta was a round Indian woman. Her straight black hair was piled up on the top her head in a complicated twist. Without breaking a beat, Geeta nodded to Joshua. "I already know what you want, so I won't waste my time asking."

Then Geeta turned to Kelly and looked at her from left to right.

"So let me tell you upfront—"

Joshua tried to interrupt Geeta before she laid down the law. Geeta was everyone's mother, and she treated everyone like her son. However, Geeta ignored him and kept right on talking to Kelly.

"Hold on, Joshua, let me finish with your young lady first."

"She's not my lady," Joshua interjected.

Geeta gave Kelly another look and then glanced at Joshua.

"You should fix that. Now, as I was saying, we have salad, but I don't think I can, in good conscious, serve it to you."

Kelly's smile widened. "Well, I guess it's a good thing. I have no intention of ordering one."

Geeta's smile spread across her whole face, and she looked back at Joshua.

"You really need to keep this one." Then she turned back to Kelly.

"Now, my little rose, tell Geeta what I can get for you."

"Can you make a triple burger?"

Geeta nodded. "Do you want cheese?"

"Yes, swiss, please. Lettuce, no tomatoes, and some sweet potato fries with mozzarella cheese if you have it."

Geeta never even took out a notepad. "Don't you worry. If Geeta doesn't have it, I'll send one of those boys to get it and bring it to you. And your drink?"

"A vanilla milkshake with whipped cream on top, and a cherry if you have it?"

"I do."

"So it seems like you have made friends with Geeta," Joshua mused.

Kelly put the napkin on her lap and folded her hands on the table. "I make it my business to make sure the cook is happy. I love food entirely too much for them to be angry at me, and I have no cooking skills at all."

"You're going to eat all of that?"

Kelly laughed. "I thought we were tossing our judginess away."

"We are, we did. I'm just saying that it was a lot of food. It was enough to give me pause."

"I'm a growing girl."

When the food came, Kelly attacked her food like a general on the battlefield. She picked up her knife and cut the burger up as if it were a pizza pie. Then she got the ketchup and squeezed a puddle of it on her plate. Every slice of the burger she dipped into the ketchup. The truly amazing part was she didn't make a mess or drop a single crumb. By the time she got to the fries, she had an assembly line of sauces. First, she dipped the fries in ketchup and then in mustard. When all of them were gone, she turned her full attention to the shake. She had finished her burger, the fries, and was halfway through her shake when she noticed he hadn't finished his burger.

"Are you okay over there? Do you need some help?"

Joshua's eyebrows went up. "Could you put anything else in there?"

Kelly smiled. "For you, I would do it if you needed me to," she teased.

He just shook his head and finished his meal. When the meal was done, and the table was cleared, he asked her the question that had been bothering him since the meeting with the principal.

"Kelly, something has been bothering me since yesterday." Kelly stopped and gave Joshua all of her attention.

"I could tell you weren't happy with the principal. And as long as I've known you, although it has been a short time, you've never hesitated to say anything to me. Why didn't you tell the principal that you wouldn't train his teachers for free or that you wouldn't be dating while you were in town?"

"Joshua, I am like everyone else. I get tired. You don't know how many places I have been where people have the same thoughts you did when you saw me. They all look at me and decide that I must be a certain way. Now when it happens, I pick and choose when I fight."

Joshua looked at Kelly, and for once, he was amazed at how insensitive he had been. "I understand what you're saying, but I think you shouldn't just take it either. I know Dorian, and he's actually a nice guy. If he thought he was being rude or pushing you to do something that you didn't want to do, he'd feel awful. You want people to give you a chance. I think you need to give them a chance, too, and let them know when you don't want to do something."

Kelly looked at him and smiled. "Joshua Case, you are just full of surprises for me.

"Kelly, I want to tell you that I am truly sorry. I was all for painting you with the ignorant brush. I was just like everyone else. When I saw you, and I saw how beautiful you were, I thought, *she has no problems.* I made the assumption that your life was as perfect as your face."

"Joshua, it is what it is. I have been in places where I had to give free training. It's what I'm good at, and I happen to love doing it, so it's not a problem."

Joshua reached out and touched her folded hands.

"But I think it is. I'll tell you the two rules that I tell my kids. Rule one: how you start will be how you finish. Rule two: you have to teach people how to treat you. It's the rule two you need help with. If you don't want to give free training, then don't."

"And when he runs back to the town and says that woman thinks she's too good to help us out, how does that go? I want to be able to do my work in town, and sometimes not just here in Sweet Blooms, but sometimes those are the trade-offs I have to make."

Kelly pulled her hands back and wrapped them around her water glass.

"How about this one? If they don't like you the way you are, they're not really your friend anyway."

Kelly looked at him and tried to keep it in, but she couldn't, and her laugh burst out.

"Is that part of the job to know those kinds of sayings?"

Joshua laughed. "Yeah, it is. Don't worry, they are tried and true wisdoms."

Joshua watched Kelly laugh, and he had started to have a whole new appreciation for her than when he started.

"You are looking so hard at me that you're going to stare a hole in me," Kelly said.

"Okay, that isn't one of the official expressions."

"No, it isn't, but it is one of the expressions that my foster mom would say to me."

Joshua noticed her expression turned sad. "Hey, what did I do?"

"It wasn't you. I was just thinking. My foster mom would have liked you."

"I remember you told the kids you were a foster kid. I would have never known. Were you in a lot of foster homes?"

"More than I could count. But Mellie Summers was the last and the best."

"Can you tell me about her?" Joshua asked.

"She was a teacher. She's the reason I became a trainer. She said I had to do something I was kin to if I wanted to be good at it," Kelly began. "It so happens I am very kin to the idea of trying to learn something, and no matter how hard you try, it doesn't get in. I think the worst part of that is when everyone around you does get it, but you don't. That's the worst."

"She sounds like a smart lady."

Kelly smiled. "She was."

Joshua's smile faded. "You said was. I'm sorry—"

Kelly waved off his apologies. "You have nothing to be sorry about. This isn't some tragic story where something bad happens to her. She passed away in her sleep of natural causes. She lived hard, and she loved harder. I'm grateful for the time I had with her and the lessons she taught me. I was with her when she left, so I was doubly blessed."

Joshua thought about Kelly and how fortunate she was. To have closure with someone you loved before they left. It was a gift. When you didn't get it, it left an unfulfilled hole in a person that slowly ate away at them. Kelly was still sad, and he wanted to do something to take away the sadness he saw in her face now.

"So, Kelly, is it true, are you really retired, or are you just taking a break in order to help us out?"

A mischievous smile came over Kelly's face.

"No, it's true. I am officially retired."

"What are you, twenty-five? To be retired at that age must be a dream."

"First of all, flattery will get you everywhere. That and chocolate. I am not twenty-five. I am thirty-something, and I think we should leave it at that. I would like to think that retirement will just be another phase in my career."

Joshua continued the conversation. He spoke about how proud he was of the kids at Castle High. He spoke about how he was so happy to be able to work with children, and it had been his only aspiration. He tried to convey to Kelly how much working with kids meant to him and how happy he was that she was going to help him help them get ahead in the world.

As time went on, the lunch crowd thinned out, and then it was time to go. Joshua paid the bill and walked Kelly to her car. Kelly turned and faced Joshua as they were standing in front of her car.

"Joshua, I wanted to thank you. I know we didn't really get any work done for the training building today, but it meant a lot to me for us to be able to talk."

Just as he was about to tell her that he was also happy that they were able to talk, she stood up on her tippy toes and then gave him a kiss on the cheek. Joshua's hand went to his cheek, and he looked down to see a smiling Kelly.

"What was that for?" said Joshua.

"It was for treating me just like any other girl, thanks."

Joshua watched as Kelly drove away. He remembered what she had said about her rules. He remembered when he said he was going to be able to keep to those rules. What he hadn't known then was that she had a personality that was more beautiful than what she looked like on the outside. The worst thing that could have happened did. Joshua Case was attracted to the one woman who was off limits to him.

Four

The next day after school, Joshua went to the barbershop. It was the original barbershop that had been built in Sweet Blooms twenty years ago. The barbershop was owned by Mr. Harold. Harold had taught his sons how to be barbers, and Harold had been taught by his father how to be a barber. The shop had five chairs. The decor inside the shop was straight out of the movies. The floors were done in large diamond shape tiles that alternated between black and white.

The walls were decorated with pictures of people who had some kind of claim to fame at one time in their lives. And, as expected, there was one wall of the shop that formed a large mirror. The mirror served a dual purpose. It was there so the person sitting in the chair could see what the barber was doing. It was also there so anyone who wanted to talk to the person in the chair could look them in the eye while he was getting his hair cut.

Walking into the barbershop, a person knew it was a holy place for men. Often, when women came into the shop, they were seen to right away so as to usher them out of the shop. Today was no different. A young mother was in the barbershop with her five-year-old son. Even though there was a line in the shop, everyone let the woman go first. After the young boy had been shaped up and the mother approved, she was immediately helped to the register and sent out the door. It was as if all the men in the shop had taken a collective sigh of relief.

Joshua knew what was going to happen; he just waited for the first person to start. He didn't have to wait long, though. Mister Harold himself told him to come and take a seat.

As a big production was made to drape the cover around him, the questions began from all sides.

"So we heard there is a new lady in town. How is she?" asked one man.

"I heard she isn't just some lady. I heard she is supposed to be the new trainer who was going to help the high schoolers," said Davy's father.

The room went quiet, and all of the men looked to Joshua. When Joshua did not answer quick enough, it was Mister Harold who jumped in.

"I don't know why all of you are beating around the bush. What we all want to know is if she really is as beautiful as everyone says she is?"

Joshua just wanted to get a haircut. He knew, though, that when he walked into the shop, he would get the third degree. If only women understood that the shop was the number one place where all men felt secure enough to gossip. The shop was a great place to get the latest information about sports. The shop was also a great place to get information about the latest stocks. The downside about the shop was it was also the place all the men talked about whoever was new in town.

"It's true, she is going to be working with the high school kids."

Joshua looked in the mirror and saw that Mr. Harold had not moved one inch to do his hair; they were all waiting for the rest of the news.

"Yes, it's true; she is attractive, but there is so much more to her than that."

The room erupted into a cacophony of voices. Joshua could hear the men joking with each other.

"The only safe man in the room is Joshua," said Davy's dad.

"Why?" asked Mr. Harold.

"Because he's the only one who isn't married. This new lady might look good, but I have to tell you so everyone can hear in case anyone decides to blab. My missus is still the most beautiful woman to me."

The other men laughed at him, and a few of the older men teased him.

"He's only saying that because he's in the first twenty. After the second twenty, what you look like doesn't even matter. The question is, can she stay with you when you're old and does she mind going with you to the doctor appointments?"

All of the men nodded. Mister Harold began to trim Joshua's hair. In the midst of all of that musing, Mister Harold tapped Joshua on the shoulder.

"Remember this advice, Joshua. Beauty fades. What really matters is having a woman who will stay with you no matter what. A good woman is a lot like a good house robe."

The other men in the shop agreed. Mister Harold went on to give his good advice.

"A good house robe may get thin. It may even get a

bit stained and not come as clean as it used to be. None of that matters. What matters is when you put it on, it still keeps you warm. A good woman is like the house robe—dependable. I know women will fuss over their appearance, but I have to tell you, it doesn't matter what my Rosy looks like. That woman has been with me when I was crazy. She's been with me when I was dumb. She never judged me, and she's never disrespected me in public. She spends a little too much at the mall, but for that, I keep the shop open another day. Even with that, I'm still coming out ahead. Rosy is a good woman worth all I have."

Joshua smiled when he saw so many nodding heads in the room. He wondered when was the last time Mr. Harold had told Rosy she was so valuable. Rosy was the head of the parent-teacher committee at Castle High. She had no idea how valued and loved she really was.

"I'm disappointed that there isn't a ball pit," Kelly said, looking around the old playhouse.

"Ball pits were banned in Sweet Blooms. They were unsanitary, and when people traveled through, it became a health hazard to maintain. One baby with an accident and you wouldn't find out until your nose led the way."

"Eww, that gives me a whole new opinion on the ball pit. To think it was on my to-do list, to jump into a ball pit. Maybe not so much now."

"It was an insurance hazard."

"It's so hard to provide clean, quality fun," Kelly teased.

Kelly and Joshua walked around the building that had been chosen to be the new location for the training site. Joshua had told her the building used to be a fun house and play pit for little kids. Lots of children would visit the place, and the only reason it closed was that the owners didn't have any children to pass the building on to. Kelly hoped that by choosing a place that had such positive historical ties, the parents would be more inclined to bring their child to get training.

They had already gone over how the building would be split up, and Kelly had laid out the creativity rooms, the tactile rooms, and the problem-solving rooms. While she understood what had to be taught, she didn't feel as though she knew the way the information needed to be presented. Then she decided to bring it up to Joshua.

"Joshua, I know how to teach, but I don't feel like I have the right stories to teach to the kids. I'm not seeing the like moments here."

"Just think back to when you were a kid and do that. I find that not much has changed when it comes to teens. They have the same fears and insecurities that I did. Guys are still interested in looking cool or whatever the word is now. They still want to be impressive to everyone, male and female. Girls still want to be adored and appreciated without having to say a word. The technology has changed, but the core motives haven't."

Kelly nodded, but she still wasn't sure. After they had finished going through the entire building, Joshua suggested they go to the neighborhood juice shop. With their juices in hand, both of them sat down at a small table on the sidewalk.

"What's wrong, Kelly?" Joshua asked. "I know the building isn't in as good a condition as we thought, but—"

"The building isn't the problem. I understand if we need to do some construction. I have the time, and I have the money to stay in Sweet Blooms for as long as I need to."

"I want to be upfront with you, Kelly. You are already the talk of the town."

Kelly smiled. "Thank you for telling me, Joshua, but I'm used to it."

"Then, unconfused Kelly, what's the problem?"

"The problem is you mentioned something in the building, and I don't have a reference for it. You told me that if I wanted to create a curriculum the teens would like, I should just remember what my childhood was like. I think you forget I didn't really have one of those childhoods. I went from foster home to foster home, and when I was finally picked up by the last foster home, I was already sixteen years old. So asking me what was it like as a teen, I don't think that's going to be the common experience."

Joshua smiled. "This is great! I mean, it's not great about you and your childhood, but this is great that we can do something that will help us both."

"Yes," Kelly said skeptically.

"I really want to understand how you make your curriculum, and you don't know what it's like to be a teen, so its harder for you to make the curriculum. Well, the answer is clear. Kelly Thomson, will you be my girlfriend for the next five days?"

She looked at him and laughed.

Joshua put his hand to his heart. "Ouch! To be rejected in high school is the worst!"

"Joshua, really?"

"Hold up before you say it's a dumb idea."

"It's a dumb idea."

Joshua laughed. "Hear me out. It's for five days only. In the next five days, I'll show you what life looks like for a teen in Sweet Blooms. It will only be the best parts. It's not like you'll get grounded or anything. Think about it. I think it's a great idea. We can work with each other, and it will be authentic for my kids."

Kelly wasn't convinced it was the way to go, but she didn't have an answer to her problem. "Let me think about it, and we can go over it tomorrow, okay?"

"No problem. Wow, it's like being in high school already."

"Why?"

"You ask a girl something, and she could never just answer and say yes or no. She always needed time."

Kelly laughed. "Tomorrow, I'll come by your place, and we can go over it."

Joshua settled up the tab and walked her in her car.

"Tomorrow?"

Kelly drove away thinking she couldn't really believe she was actually considering making Joshua her boyfriend. What thirty year old even said the word boyfriend?

When Sally had heard something in the middle of the night, she had given her mother a call, but her mother was unable to come home. As part of the Let's Keep Children Safe patrol and the emergency tree,

Joshua Case was the first one on the list. He'd given his number out to his kids and to their parents. That way, if any of his kids felt insecure or like they needed help, they could call him.

This was a part of the initiative that he had started two years ago. With so many children feeling isolated, and with Sweet Blooms having so little funding, Joshua felt as though he had to do something. Three years ago, they'd almost lost a child to depression. Everyone in town knew something needed to be done, but no one had any ideas. When Joshua came up with the emergency tree and the initiative—that a student or parent could call—and he volunteered to man it, the town was relieved.

Tonight, Sally had been in one of those situations. As he had promised, he came straight over. He went in and checked the house, then checked the windows and doors.

"I'm sorry, Mr. Case. I know it's late," sixteen-year-old Sally Jeffries said as she opened the door for Joshua.

Joshua told her it was fine. It was midnight when Sally had called Joshua. Sally Jeffries' mom worked the night shift as a nurse in the Cordero hospital. Sally and her mom lived alone in a rental house that was at the end of a dark block. The neighborhood wasn't bad. The problem was at night. Sally got scared, and she had a smaller sister to look after as well.

Joshua had created an unofficial protocol. First, he called Sally's mom at the hospital. When she answered the phone, he motioned Sally over and told her to tell her mother that he was in the house and he was checking it.

Joshua walked through the three bedroom house.

He could tell that Sally's mother truly adored her girls. On all of the walls, there were pictures of them having fun at amusement parks, laughing at parties, and some of the dreaded school photos had made it to the walls.

His house had been like this before the Jordan incident. His mother had been so vibrant and outgoing. Every year she planned a vacation for the family to go on, and it was always something new and something educational.

He and Jordan would look for places next to large amusement parks. If the park was within a certain amount of miles and there was the time, they always made it. He and Jordan were, as they called themselves, the tag team that couldn't be beaten.

The last room that Joshua checked had Sally's little sister. She was all tucked in to her bed that was shaped a Barbie car. As time went on, Joshua had thought about having a family, but he needed to find a missus first.

On his way back to the kitchen where he had left Sally, he checked all of the windows to make sure they were shut, and he checked all of the doors to make sure they were locked. When he got back to the kitchen, Sally gave him the phone back.

He spoke to Sally's mother and reported everything he had done and then hung up the phone.

"Okay, Sally, I've checked it all."

He could see she was still nervous and she wanted to say something. Part of Joshua's protocol was to ask if the teen felt okay. If she still wasn't feeling okay, he had permission from her mom to call the police, and they could send a female officer to stay with her. It was one of the benefits of living in a small town. When the officers showed up, you already knew them.

"Mr. Case, do you think Ms. Thomson gets scared?"

When Sally asked that question, the picture that jumped into his head was one of Kelly standing with a shield and sword, daring the enemy to come near. He shook off the picture and answered to the best of his ability.

Joshua smiled. "Yes, even she gets scared sometimes. It's part of what makes us all human."

"I don't mean here when I'm alone. I mean like when a person goes to school." Joshua wanted to ask her what was she afraid of, but he had to wait. If he had learned anything working with his kids, it was that they would tell you when they were ready.

"You heard her tell everyone she was in a foster home. I think she was scared a lot because she didn't have a home."

Sally looked at him and then said, "Maybe, but when you're pretty, everybody likes you, so you don't really have a good reason to be scared."

Just when Joshua thought he could address it, she stopped talking and said, "Thank you for coming out."

When Sally asked him if he wanted to wait inside until her mother came home, he said no. Instead, he told her he would be sitting in his truck until her mother came home.

As Joshua pushed his seat back as far as it would go, he thought about his schedule tomorrow. He was packed with meetings from eleven to three. This call couldn't have come at a worse time, but he shook it off. This was the work that was important. He was also supposed to see Kelly tomorrow. To find out if she wanted to be his girlfriend. The question and the thought brought a smile to his face.

He lay down in his truck and waited. In four hours, Sally's mom would show up and knock on the window of his car to let him know he could go home, take a shower, and go to work. His mother often told him he was doing too much, but she understood the beast that drove him to do this. As long as he was in the school, if it was humanly possible, he would make sure that Castle High School didn't lose any more students to depression or suicide.

As he closed his eyes in his truck, his hand went to the half-heart necklace that was around his throat. .

"We won't lose any more, Jordan. I promise I'm on watch." Those were the mutterings of Joshua Case as he drifted off to sleep.

Five

Kelly wasn't sure what to expect when she went to Joshua's house. At first, she thought she would see a house dedicated to children. The house she saw was a house that could have been on any block. The lawn was well manicured. She could tell someone made sure there were no weeds on this front lawn. The house itself was set back from the road. It was white with blue trim. The only color that graced the front of this house were the potted plants that were hanging on the porch. In those pots were an array of colorful plants that spilled out of them.

Today was the day they had agreed to meet. It was also the day she was supposed to give him an answer about being his girlfriend. She had been thinking about it ever since he made the suggestion.

She walked up to the white steps that led to his front door. When she pushed the doorbell, the Sound of Music theme song played. Then the door opened just as it was ending.

"You've got an interesting doorbell," she said.

He smiled, although it looked a bit sad. "Yes, my brother picked it. Come in."

He stepped back so that she could walk through the door. As she walked by him, she could smell the soap scent coming off of his body. She noticed he was wearing shorts, and she had to admit, with muscular legs like his, he should probably wear shorts more often.

"I'm glad you made it. I wondered if my directions would be a help or a hindrance?" she asked.

"Yes, the directions were fine. Take a seat."

The outside of the house might have looked like everyone else's, but once you were inside, you knew a man lived here. The furniture was large and oversized. The colors in the house were blues and natural woods. If nothing else gave it away, the TV in the living room was huge. The television took center stage so that no matter where you sat in the living room, you would be able to see it. She walked in, and a smile played along her lips.

He walked into the living room and went to a large oversized chair. She could tell it was his favourite chair. On the right side was an end table, and there were some rings on the table that suggested it had seen more than its fair share of cups. On the armrest of the chair was a sleeve that held two remote controls. In front of the chair, there was a little ottoman where he could put his feet up. When he sat down in the chair, she could see his whole demeanor relaxed. Kelly had opted to sit on the sofa directly across from the chair.

"So I want you to know I have been thinking about what you said. About you being my boyfriend, as crazy as that sounds."

She could see Joshua smiling as she spoke.

"Before I make a decision like that, I want to ask you a question."

"Go ahead."

"I always think it's very important to understand why people do things. I know that you are really dedicated to the children. And everyone says that you have a lot of knowledge when it comes to the children. What I want to know is what made you decide to do this. I told you about my foster mom and how she was my inspiration, but you haven't told me what motivated you to be here."

Joshua went still in his chair. For a moment she thought he wasn't even going to answer the question. Whatever had been his motivation wasn't as nice as her foster mom. Just when she was about to tell him to forget about it and move on to another subject, he spoke.

He gave her a sad smile. "Forgive me if I seem a little slow to speak about it. It's just that it's been so long, and for a moment, I forgot you aren't from Sweet Blooms, so you wouldn't know."

Kelly moved to the edge of her seat. "I'm sorry, Joshua. If it's something that is personal, you don't have to share it. And if it's something that is painful, I definitely don't want you to have to relive anything that's unpleasant."

Joshua took a deep breath. "No, you have the right of it, and you were open with me." Kelly waited for him to collect himself.

"It's not that I don't want to tell you. The real question for me is, where do I start. So let's see. You probably would need to know how it began. In a town like Sweet Blooms, twins are a big deal. I had an older brother, by two minutes; his name was Jordan. Jordan and I did everything together. Even though we were identical twins, we had very different personalities.

The whole town adored us, and to everyone else, it looked like we were the perfect family. But as time went on, Jordan just wasn't happy. There would be days when he wouldn't come out of his room. My parents tried to do what they could, but they just didn't understand what was wrong."

Kelly watched Joshua as he began to tell the story. After a few moments, he stood up and started to pace in front of the couch as he was talking.

"Anyway, the short of it was that Jordan was diagnosed with depression. We had tried the medications. In fact, I have to say that my parents really did the best they could with what they knew. One day, my mom and dad took us on a family outing, hoping it would help lighten things up."

Kelly heard the slight hitch in Joshua's voice, and she prepared herself for the inevitable end to this story.

"We went out to the picnic grounds, and there was a lake. I asked my parents if Jordan and I could go swimming, and they said yes. We both knew how to swim, and we had taken a floating raft just in case.

Jordan and I were racing in the lake. I swam out too fast and too far and caught a cramp. Jordan saw me in the water, and he swam over to me and brought the floating raft. He put me on the raft and then he pushed it toward the shore. I thought he was right behind me. I thought he was swimming behind the raft and that's why it was going toward the shore. But at some point, he just wasn't there. No one could say if he was tired or exhausted or what had happened;

the only thing anyone knew was he wasn't there, and he had saved me."

Kelly knew where the story was going, but still, hearing him say it made the horror real.

"You don't know, do you?" she asked.

Joshua shook his head.

"I would like to remember Jordan as a hero. I wish I could believe that he had just given everything he could to save me. But I was his twin. I was the one he talked to at night. I was the one he would tell when he just wanted to go away. So I relive that day, and I think *if only I had known more.* If only we had been more informed, we could have offered him the things he needed, and I could have some closure that the day he saved me, he was a hero and not a desperate child looking for a way out."

Kelly wasn't a very emotional person. She had been through too much in her own personal life to empathize with what other people thought were concerns. But right now, the only thing she wanted to do was to hold Joshua and tell him that he wasn't to blame. She wanted to go back in time and hold that little boy and tell him not to feel guilty about Jordan's death. She wanted to tell him that people make their own decisions, and sometimes they forget they leave people who love them behind to deal with the consequences of those decisions.

"It sounds stupid and useless to say this, but I'm so sorry," she said.

"It's not stupid, and I want you to know it's appreciated. At any rate, what wound up happening was I became the twin that survived."

"How did you and your family deal with it? How did you all deal with the doubt?"

Kelly held out her hand, and Joshua walked over and sat beside her on the couch. She rubbed his hand and waited for him to speak.

"We didn't. My parents never discussed it. My father wouldn't talk about it, and my mother decided that I could have whatever I wanted."

"And you, Joshua? How did you deal with it?"

"Afterwards, I read everything I could find about teenage depression. Then, as I got older, I decided I wanted to make sure that no one else went through the doubt and the pain that my family went through with Jordan. So I learned everything I could. I studied to become a guidance counselor, and now that's where I'm at—in school, helping troubled teens and being there for them the way that I wish someone had been there for Jordan."

It was now so clear to Kelly why Joshua was so defensive of his kids. She listened to everything that he had to say. The one thing she hadn't heard him say was how he had dealt with the guilt. If she understood everything, no one had even taken him to see a counselor or to even look at his survivor's guilt. As she listened to him talk, she wondered if he even knew that he was carrying around the guilt from Jordan still.

"I bet you weren't expecting to hear that kind of story as my inspiration. On a lighter note, I want you to know I have thought about our problem."

Kelly raised her eyebrow. "Our problem?"

Joshua smiled. "Yes, our problem. You don't know how to be a teen, and I don't really know how to organize the training. I know one day I'll be here by myself after you've done the implementing, and I want to be able to grow the program you start. To do that,

I think I need to learn some project ways. And I have it on good authority that you are the best to learn from."

"Well, I can't argue with the facts, as you've put them out, but spell it out for me."

"I'll be your boyfriend, and you'll teach me the ways of training."

"I don't know, Joshua, this whole boyfriend thing seems so personal."

"Look at it more like we're just helping each other out. It'll be temporary, and before you know it, it'll be over. Come on, give it a shot."

"It's crazy, but I'll do it."

"That's the spirit. Look, you are already on your road to living life as a teen. What did you say? It was crazy, but you're going to do it anyway. You've got step one already figured out."

Kelly pulled her hand back and moved over on the couch. "Okay, we've decided everything. We can start tomorrow."

Joshua smiled. "I think we should seal our deal with a kiss."

Kelly looked at him incredulously. "What?"

Joshua shrugged. "I'm just saying now that we're going out and all, we should commemorate this moment."

She folded her arms over her chest and laughed. "Well, in the words of a very wise guidance counselor, my answer to that is that I plan to start the way I intend to go. I don't plan on giving out kisses to you, so I'm not starting it now."

Joshua pretended to grab his chest as if he were hurt. "Already saying the dreaded word."

Kelly laughed. "Which word would that be?"

"No."

"You are crazy, and I'm leaving before my common sense comes back, and I dump you."

She left and got back in her car. As she drove back to her cottage, she thought about everything that had been said. Nothing that was worth doing was ever easy. She was seeing Joshua in a new light. A new light that was moving him from the client category into the man category. She had told Joshua about her rules. She needed to make sure she kept to her rules and didn't fall for the client.

Kelly thought she would miss her gym. She thought that, being in a little town with a whole lot of sweet shops, the only thing she would be lifting would be a cupcake or two to her mouth. She was very wrong. Kelly knew all about the hustle and bustle that went into creating a training program. What she didn't know was all of the planning and work that went into preparing the building to put the training program in it.

The morning started at five thirty with her and Joshua meeting at the building. It was maybe twenty minutes later that the construction crew showed up as well. The first meeting was with the construction foreman.

The foreman was a nice man. Kelly thought he must be about five foot even. The laugh lines on his face said he was in his mid-sixties. She thought this conversation would be very slow and very short. She was wrong on both accounts. The man had the agility of a chimpanzee and the strength of a bear.

He wanted to go over where and how many rooms there were to be in the building. Kelly had to learn all about load bearing beams that couldn't be moved and about keeping the studs in the wall a foot apart. Once they had figured out how many rooms there were going to be, then they had to figure out what was going to go in those rooms so the electrician could come in.

Kelly was impressed with Joshua. When the construction foreman said something she didn't understand, Joshua would stop him and explain everything to her. At one point they all got up and did a walkthrough of the building. Kelly thought that Joshua's patience was above and beyond what she would ever have.

The clock had just rolled around to nine o'clock when Yolanda came in from the county courthouse. Kelly thought there would be some sort of break here. Yolanda was a lovely woman dressed in a suit. The building had no air conditioner, and the makeshift table was in the heat. After the foreman, she thought this would be addressed quickly. Of course, she knew Joshua and congratulated him on the project. In her hand, Yolanda had all of the documents they needed to have filed and signed in the courthouse before any of the construction could begin.

By the time Yolanda left, Kelly was ready to nominate Joshua for sainthood. It appeared that no matter what town a person went to, the bureaucracy was still practiced. Kelly had no idea how many permits it took just to get one building built. There was a permit to build on the weekdays. There was a permit in order to remove garbage. There was a permit to get a permit so that someone could go and put cones around the construction area to make sure no one got hurt. The permits went on and on.

It took Kelly and Joshua two hours to go over every license and every permit. Joshua checked and double checked everything so that there would be no stops in the construction. After Yolanda left, a young woman named Penny came in. Kelly wasn't surprised; she also knew Joshua. By this point, Kelly had given up on getting any break whatsoever. She knew now there had to be something in the water because they were all so happy and helpful, even though this was proving to be the longest procedure ever.

Penny needed to go over all of the legal documents and all the disclaimers that they needed to set up and file at the courthouse. She also needed to go over the information packet that would be given to every family that wanted their child to participate in the training center.

Two hours later, they were done with Penny, and the foreman came in to ask them if they wanted to do a walk around the property because he had some questions. At that point, Kelly would have done anything just to never see another piece of paper for the rest of the day. When they started to walk through the grounds, Kelly got a chance to truly appreciate the task at hand. When she looked back at the building they were converting, she realized it would need a whole new overhaul.

The foreman was pointing out places where they could set up picnic benches for the kids to eat outside. He also asked her if she thought she would be doing any teaching outside. They could block off a place and set up a tent for her if she wanted.

There were so many options and so many choices. Through it all, Joshua was with her, offering his advice. Letting her know what the thought. When she wanted to put the tent near the water, he told her maybe it should be a little farther so if anything was in the water, it wouldn't go into her tent for shade. She wanted to ask what would do that but decided ignorance was bliss.

Kelly had to admit that she was still a little nervous about this whole boyfriend-girlfriend thing, but she had spent the whole day with Joshua, and he was still the same. Maybe she had been overthinking the whole thing.

The second and fourth Thursday of every month was visitation day. His mother, Patricia Case, was living at an assisted living home. The home was outside of Sweet Blooms, so it took him about two hours to get to it. It was more like an all-inclusive resort. When he had first brought her to the place, he joked with her that maybe he should move in with her.

After Joshua's father died, she didn't want to stay in the house anymore. She said the memories were just too much for her. So on the second and the fourth Thursday of every month, Joshua went to see his mother.

"You came," Patricia said as Joshua walked into her room. She didn't smile at him when he walked in, but she never did. She was sitting in a chair facing the window. Joshua had made sure she had an apartment on the first floor that faced the inner courtyard. The home always kept the flowers in bloom, and the sun shone in the room for at least half the day. Joshua figured if there were days his mother didn't make it outside, or when she couldn't make it outside, at least she would still have the opportunity to feel the sun on her face.

"Of course I came. I told you I'd visit."

Patricia had been at the facility for the last eight years. During that time, Joshua had come to know all of the staff. They were helpful and called him if his mother needed anything. He'd had to enlist their help because he knew his mother wouldn't call him for anything.

Today she was dressed in blue pants and a white top. Her hair was done up in a knot in the back of her head. There were some days when he came where she was still in her night clothes. If she had on outside clothes, it was a better day than most. The staff didn't dress or undress his mother. She was still able to take care of herself when she wanted to.

"Why do you come here anyway? I want you to go and live," she pleaded with him.

"Mom, I'm happy where I am."

"You're still in that town. How can you be happy?"

Joshua never knew what mood his mother would be in. He hoped she would break out of her melancholy mood, but nothing was guaranteed. It didn't seem like it would happen today, either.

"I spoke with the nurses and your doctor. They think you should get out more. You don't need to stay in your room. Do you have enough pocket money?" Joshua asked.

She didn't even answer him. When he went to sit in front of her, she seemed to look right through him.

"We're opening up a training center in Sweet Blooms. It will be for kids who need help."

He reached out and touched her lap. For a moment, she smiled. She reached her frail hand out and caressed his cheek.

"Jordan, my sweet Jordan." Then, when she ran her hands through his hair, the smile fell away. "Do you know how I used to tell the difference between the two of you? One had curls, and one didn't. Your hair is straight." Her hand fell away, and Joshua stood up to leave.

"I'll be back in two weeks, mom. Do you want me to bring you anything?" he asked, trying to keep the hurt out of his voice. Just when he was sure she wouldn't say anything, she spoke.

"Joshua?"

"Yes, mom?"

"I'm sorry."

"For?"

"I'm sorry we didn't talk about it. Even now, I can't say it. I'm sorry."

Trying to change the subject and keep her more engaged, Joshua said the first thing he could think of.

"Aunt Ann is coming."

His mother looked away.

"She'd really like you to talk to her."

"I have nothing to say."

He nodded and then he left, saying goodbye to the nurses as he went by. Maybe when the center was done, he would bring her out so she could see it. She might even be able to meet some of the kids by then. Maybe.

Six

Today had been declared an off day. Kelly had plans. She was going to find out if there was a spa anywhere and get herself a manicure and pedicure. If she had time and found an open appointment, she was even thinking about getting a massage. The birds had been chirping since about six, but Kelly had just rolled over when she got a text. She reached over and picked up her phone to see who it was.

Joshua: *Are you up?*

Kelly: *I'm up enough, why?*

Joshua: *Your boyfriend wants to take you out today.*

Kelly smiled as she sat up in her bed and looked at her phone.

Kelly: *Really, and where are we going?*

Joshua: *That's part of the surprise because you are thrilled that I'm taking you out and paying. LOL*

Kelly: *I've got my own money, so why don't I take you out and we can go to a nice dinner?*

Joshua: *Stop crushing my budding man-pride. Come on, let's go out.*

Kelly saw all of her spa plans going down the drain.

Kelly: *Okay, I'll go out with you.*

Kelly had just put her phone down, and it wasn't even ten minutes later that she heard her doorbell ring. Disheveled and still with her nightshirt on, she went to the door. When she opened the door, on the other side was Joshua smiling from ear to ear.

"What are you doing here? We just got off the phone," she complained.

"You are absolutely right; we did just get off the phone, and I came right over."

"I'm not ready. I just got up out of bed," she exclaimed.

"It's okay. I know I'm going to have to wait for you to get ready, but I don't have anything else to do but hang out with you, so I'll sit on the couch and wait," he said as he walked in, sat on the couch, and pulled out his phone.

"You know this makes no sense, right?"

Joshua kept his smile up and nodded in agreement. Kelly didn't even try to talk to him; she just went in to get dressed. Twenty minutes later, Kelly came out dressed in blue jeans and a pink polo shirt.

"You didn't tell me where we were going, so I hope I'm dressed appropriately."

When the both of them went outside, Kelly didn't see Joshua's truck. The only odd thing she did see was a pickup truck in front of her house. It was old, but it had a flatbed. She imagined someone must use it to haul garbage or dirt around. All the windows were rolled down. And it looked as though it could use a paint job. When Joshua started to walk toward the truck, she immediately stopped in her tracks.

"Where's your truck?" she asked.

"Mr. Harold is going to borrow my truck for the day,

and I figured so we would have the full teen experience, I'd borrow Mr. Harold's truck."

"You know I have a car, right?"

"I do."

Kelly got into the truck and closed the door. As soon as she sat down, she thought she smelled something funny.

"Do you smell that?" she asked.

Joshua just smiled, and he started the truck up and off they went.

Joshua had been driving for about forty minutes when finally he stopped in front of the zoo. Kelly looked up at the side and then looked at Joshua.

"You have got to be kidding me."

"Nope, I'm not kidding you. The reason we are going to the zoo is because I want to take you out on a date. But I don't have a lot of money. And today, getting into the zoo is free."

Kelly was prepared to hate the zoo. As soon as they walked in, Joshua was all smiles. The first thing they did was take a ride on an elephant. She almost fell off twice. But Joshua grabbed her around her waist to keep her in the saddle.

When they got off of the elephant, she turned him and told him how much fun it was. After the ride, they offered pictures, and Kelly kept one of them where she had her eyes shut because she knew she was going to fall off.

As the day went on, they went on more and more rides. With each ride, she discovered Joshua had already been on it. When they came upon the one rollercoaster in the park, Joshua got in line. Kelly stopped.

"Hey, what's wrong?"

Kelly was embarrassed to tell him, but it couldn't be helped. "I'm afraid of heights."

"Ah, that could be a problem on a roller coaster."

She waited for him to make fun of her. It wouldn't be the first time. Instead, he suggested they walk to the other end of the rollercoaster; it would take them to the food court. She was taken aback by his consideration. When they got ready to start the walk, he offered his hand.

Kelly looked at it questioningly.

"Its common for couples to hold hands." She placed her hand in his, and after a while, she barely remembered.

They walked all over the zoo. And the more they walked, the more they talked. Finally, it was time to get something to eat. They stopped at a hot dog stand. Kelly had to admit she was having fun. She got to see a whole new side of Joshua. When she thought about the day, there were moments where his kindness and consideration had caught her off guard. She was pleasantly surprised.

Joshua went to go get the food, and he brought it back to the table. At first, she thought he was being very rude. It was so at odds with how he had been all day long.

"Why didn't you tell me that I needed to get my own hot dog?" she said as she got ready to stand up.

Joshua reached to stop her from going, laughing all the while.

"I didn't mean for you to get your own. I thought we would share."

Kelly looked at the hot dog and then at Joshua; she began to laugh.

"You can't be serious! I know we are doing the couple thing, but I have money."

"Kelly, I'm sensing you have an issue with sharing," he said with a smile.

"Sharing is when we don't have enough money," she said.

"Or, and wait for it, sharing could be a way that we show we are together."

She looked at the hot dog and then looked at him. She sat down, reaching out and pulling his hands into hers. Then she turned her face to him and smiled her best smile.

"You can be my boyfriend until food is involved, and then we go our separate ways!"

Kelly heard Joshua laughing at her as she went to the stand to get her food.

When Kelly came back, she had two loaded hot dogs and a side of fries. Joshua laughed as she raised her eyebrow and began to eat. After she had finished eating, she had to ask him a question.

"So I have to ask you a question. I've traveled just about everywhere, and the one thing that always gets me about small towns is that everyone knows everyone. Is that true in Sweet Blooms?"

Joshua thought about it and then nodded yes. "It's true. Most of the time, it's a great thing. I went away to school at a university that was right outside a big city. It would always seem crazy to me that all of the city people were ready to pay an arm and a leg for the life we have here in Sweet Blooms. They talked about knowing their neighbors. Making sure their kids were safe, and then when they thought they had it, they put a gate around it."

Kelly laughed with him. "I guess everyone wants what they don't have, right?"

"I remember you said you were a foster child. Did you ever try to find out who your real parents were?"

"I didn't. When I was younger, I used to think my life would be just like little orphan Annie. That went away after the first month in foster homes."

"Were the foster homes bad?"

Kelly waved him off. "I'm not going to complain about the people who took me in and gave me a place no matter how long or short. They didn't have to do anything. To be fair, I wasn't the easiest child anyway."

"You?! I never would have guessed it."

"Haha. Well, to finish answering your question, after a certain age, I stopped dreaming about it, and I went on with my life. I thought if I did find them, it would all be so awkward. If they wanted to find me, they could. They have the advantage of knowing where they left me."

By the end of the day, Kelly had to admit she had had a good time. Even the drive in the old smelling truck wasn't so bad going back home.

When they finally got to her house, she was about to open the door when Joshua asked her to wait. Then she saw Joshua get out of the cab and run around the front of the truck so he could open her door.

"I had a good time today, Joshua," she said.

"Me too. I know now never to get between you and food, but everything else is a go," he said with a smile.

They had both said good night, and Kelly was walking down the path to her house when she stopped. Joshua was standing by her closed truck door. She supposed he was watching her to make sure she made it safely into her home. She took that opportunity to walk back to Joshua.

He looked concerned when she stopped in front of him. "Did you forget some—"

She cut him off when she wrapped her arms around his neck and pulled him down so she could kiss him. It was a long kiss, but it was enough for her to realize it felt right.

When they separated, he began to speak, but she placed her fingers over his lips.

"Don't ask me because I don't have the answer. Thank you for an amazing date."

She didn't look back. Once she was in her cottage, she closed the door and then leaned against it. She didn't move until she heard the truck pull away, which wasn't for another five minutes.

She might not know the finer mechanics of being a teen, but she knew she had just made a discovery that could ruin everything. Kelly Thomson liked Joshua Case in a way too personal kind of way.

Joshua was walking on cloud nine. Today had been one of the best days of his life. It just didn't get any better. He smiled and thought things were looking up for him. He had dropped off Mr. Harold's truck and picked his up. When he pulled up to his house, there was a cab unloading some bags. He didn't have to see the occupant to know who it was. Life had been so hectic that he hadn't been looking at the calendar. Every year, for a week, his aunt came to stay with him and visit with his mother.

He had pulled up behind the taxi and cut his lights. Joshua knew. All of the pleasure he felt was squeezed out of him, and in its place was a dark hole of duty. There was no way to escape it or his past. Ann was his mother's fraternal twin.

Seven

"Joshua, you have good timing."

It always jolted him hearing his name coming from his Aunt Ann. While it was true she didn't look exactly like his mother, she did sound like her. Ever practical, she wore a pair of dark pants and a khaki top. She also had on a pair of dark shoes. For as long as Joshua could remember, Ann had never worn sneakers. When he'd asked her about it one day, she had said, "Sneakers are for runners, athletes, and teenagers. I'm not in any one of those categories, so I don't need sneakers."

"Ann," he said as he stood on the sidewalk.

It was like a standoff. Ann stood in the middle of the sidewalk. She opened her arms and waited for him to come to her. She wouldn't move, and she wouldn't meet him halfway. People were often deceived by her short bob haircut, and the way everything on her was so coordinated. If his mother was country, Ann made sure she was considered anything but.

Ann was sixty, the same age as his mother, but she looked younger. She attributed her skin to her better living, of course. She stood a full five foot six.

So they wouldn't be out in the street all night, Joshua went to his aunt and gave her a hug.

"It's good that you're here. I tried to call you, but you didn't pick up. You weren't home."

"No, I gave you my cell phone number so you could reach me."

"Yes, cell phones. Well, I didn't memorize your cell phone number so I couldn't call it. You know, depending on your phone to remember all of your numbers is a true way to lose your memory."

"Let me take your bags."

"You look surprised to see me, and you smell funny."

Joshua almost laughed out loud with that one.

"I was out with a friend."

"Oh, where do you guys hang out now?"

"It wasn't a guy."

"You went out with a woman dressing and smelling like that?" And then it all came back to Joshua why he never called Ann or tried to include her in things even though she lived only twenty miles away. In fact, he wouldn't have even let her come over if it hadn't been one of the things his mother had asked him to do before she went into the home.

"She didn't mind." Then he heard her mutter something about women in small towns. Joshua smiled when he thought about Kelly being called a girl from a small town. After all of the bags had been brought into the house, Ann went into the living room and sat down.

"Well, I'm here, and I'll be seeing your mother starting tomorrow. What are you going to do for your birthday?"

"The same thing I do every year—nothing."

"You know we are family."

Joshua turned and looked at her. "Yes, we are family for one week out of the year."

"That's your choice. I'd love for you to visit."

"I think it's better this way. I can get you set up in your room."

"Thank you for that."

Joshua knew it wouldn't matter what he said. When it came to his aunt, he could never win. Every year she would make the trip of mercy to see his mother. Things had gotten so bad that his aunt had stopped referring to his mother as her sister.

There was so much that was unsaid between him and Ann. Even the room she stayed in was a barrier between both of them. Aunt Ann always stayed in Jordan's old room. Joshua knew if he could just survive the next seven days, it would all be okay.

"Time! Everyone sit in your seat," Kelly called out. "I'll do my first assessment."

While the building was being built, the school had offered Kelly the use of two classrooms. In the classroom, she had set up two tasks for the three groups to do. The first task was for the children to figure out how to get a car across a bridge. They were given the car, which was a weighted Lego car. The other task was for them to build the bridge. They were also given a budget, and each member of the team had to participate in the planning of the bridge.

The testing was actually going very well. In the next creativity test, she was going to include things like how to move animals from one side of the zoo to the other.

She also thought about throwing in some budgeting problems, like when people wanted to go out on a date, but they only had a certain amount of money.

She could see that the task were working well for group one; group three was the problem. Every time she turned around, group three was taking too much time looking at her and not enough time doing any of their work.

Kelly went over to the third group and gathered them around their project.

"What's the problem, guys? Do you need help? Or was there some part of the exercise you didn't understand?"

One of the taller young men smiled. "I think we need you to help us out. We need extra attention." The rest of the members in his group laughed with him. Kelly looked at the boys, and then she looked at everyone else in the room. There was always one smart guy in the group. It didn't matter if they were teens or if they were adults; there was always one.

"I have just the thing for you in the other room." The boys followed her into the next room, and she knew the other teams would be looking as well. She was hoping that this wasn't going to be necessary, but she tried to prepare for everything.

"I realize you are getting excused from class and your teacher will want to see what you were able to do in this trial. Since the first two tasks were too hard, you can do the primer tasks."

The boys stepped into the room, and the only thing they could see were large Lego blocks.

"I think we're in the wrong room," snickered one of the boys.

Kelly shook her head. "No, this is the right room. Do you see all of the Lego blocks all around?"

The boys nodded yes. The older boy in the group was still laughing, but some of the other kids in the group were getting a little nervous.

"I want you to build the alphabet using the same color blocks for each letter. When you are done, we will take a picture, and that way, we can make sure you get credit for being away from class."

At first, the boy didn't believe her, but when Kelly didn't move, and the other kids stopped laughing as well, he knew she was serious.

"We can't do this and then show our teacher," he exclaimed.

"Well, you have a choice. You can either build this, or you can just go back to your classroom."

Kelly ignored the other students who were trying to keep their laughter down while they looked at the group three trying to figure their way out of the mess they'd gotten themselves in. When it was clear Kelly wasn't going to budge, the boys began to build the letters.

Kelly reviewed everyone's work, and then she stepped out of the classroom. Joshua was waiting for her outside the classroom.

"I saw you in there, and that was pretty good."

"Do you know those boys?"

"Yeah, they are often in trouble in one way or another."

"Are you satisfied that I might know a way or two to deal with people who look at my face and think my head is empty?"

"Ouch! I can see that I have nothing to worry about.

But you can't blame me for being concerned that you have so many people who will fall over themselves for you."

"Well, in case you haven't heard, I've got myself someone new in my life."

"You're seeing someone in Sweet Blooms?" he asked.

"You look worried," she teased.

"I'm not worried. I was just thinking I didn't know that—"

Kelly had to stop him before she started laughing. "I'm talking about you, silly. Remember, we're a couple; you're my boyfriend. I can't be doing this right if you forget so quickly."

Kelly watched him as he tried to recover and find himself again, and she decided to spare him. "Off with you. I've got work to do, and so do you."

Aunt Ann had decided that today was a good day to go to the school to see Joshua. When she arrived at the school, the security guard was very helpful. When she told him that she was looking for Joshua, he smiled at her and took her to his office. The door was closed, but she decided to wait.

Ann looked around the office and found all the colors to be very drab. It appeared as though the walls were just varying shades of gray. The floor had gray speckled tiles, and the doors were suspiciously grey as well. On the walls, he had them covered with posters about teen depression, teen problems, speaking out, and how other people would be there to help you. As far as she was concerned, the whole office was just a temple to the things that could go wrong in a teen's life.

Finally, the door opened, and Joshua came out with a young man standing right behind him.

"Ann, what are you doing here?"

"I thought I would come by and maybe we could do lunch. Or, at the very least, I could see where you work." He turned from her and leaned down to whisper something in the young man's ear. Whatever he said made him smile, and he left the room.

"Joshua, don't you think that was very rude to whisper while I'm in the room? A person might think you were talking about me."

"We were, and that was why we whispered."

Ann sighed. "I'm trying, Joshua."

"I agree, you are trying, but you're doing it on your time. I have appointments to keep for today. So today is not a good day for me. Why don't we try it tomorrow or next week?"

"I'm gone next week!"

"Let me look at my calendar." That was the end of that, and Joshua disappeared from the room. She stood in his office and let out a sigh. A few moments later, a woman walked into the office.

"Joshua, I was thinking and—"

She stopped as soon as she saw Ann and gave her a smile that invited Ann to smile back.

"Hello," the young woman said.

"Hello to you. If you're looking for Joshua, he just left for an appointment."

"Ahh, I figured. I wasn't sure, but I wanted to talk to him about some things, and I was going to bribe him with lunch."

Ann was refreshed with the girl's honesty.

"I forgot myself. Where are my manners? My name is Ann Glen. I'm Joshua's aunt."

"I'm Kelly Thomson. I'm the independent trainer they brought in for the school training center."

"Well, it's good to meet you."

"You as well."

"Well, I'm done for the day. I know Joshua isn't here, but would you like to go to lunch?"

Ann smiled. "I'd love to."

Kelly had her own car, so they drove it from the school to the juice shop. Both of them had decided on the way that they weren't really hungry, so just stopping by for some smoothies would be great. Ann was impressed with Kelly's looks and her confidence.

When they arrived, it appeared as though the barrister knew exactly who Kelly was. They were seated outside the restaurant as the sun set behind them.

"So, what brings you to Sweet Blooms?" asked Kelly.

"Oh, I've come to visit Joshua, and I've also come to visit my sister, Joshua's mom. Family can be complicated, and sometimes Joshua is so busy we don't really have time to talk to each other."

"It must be hard for you both," Kelly said.

"It is. Not many people recognize that," Ann said.

"Loss affects everyone in the family. Families are already such complicated animals as it is," Kelly replied.

"How do you know Joshua?"

"Ah, I met him doing the training project for the kids. He's been very helpful, and he's very giving of his time. He was kind enough to take me out yesterday."

"Ah, so you're the friend."

Kelly nodded. "I'm guilty. It was me."

Ann took a second look at Kelly. All of a sudden, it was very clear why Joshua wanted to be with her. Kelly was not only a beautiful woman, she was smart as well as sensitive. Kids liked to tell themselves all sorts of stories when they weren't ready to hear the truth. They might be friends now, but she could see how easy it would be for Joshua to fall in love with Kelly.

"I'm afraid that Joshua doesn't make a lot of time for me."

"Do you know what he does?"

"Of course, he's a guidance counselor. He works with the teachers to help the kids."

"Joshua does more than that. Joshua is responsible for setting up a majority of the programs that help the teens in Castle High. He also volunteers his time to help teens if they need some more help with their homework, or if they just need to talk to someone. Joshua is also an advocate for the kids at Castle High. It's because of him that I'm here. He went to Ethan Young and asked him if he would help to build a training center for the kids."

"I didn't know he did so much," Ann said. What Ann found more interesting was that Kelly knew everything that Joshua did even though she was a recent transplant to Sweet Blooms.

"I know dealing with family can be difficult. But I also know that Joshua is a good and fair person."

Ann saw Kelly look at her watch, and then she called the waitress over to settle the bill. When Ann tried to contribute to the bill, Kelly refused to take her money. She told Ann that coming to lunch was a favor to her so she wouldn't have to eat alone. Kelly asked Ann if she needed to be dropped off anywhere, but Ann declined.

She told her she wanted to do some shopping in town so she would have gifts to take to her sister.

Joshua went back to his office. He was slow to enter, not sure what he would find. He was concerned that when he did go to his office, his Aunt Ann would still be there waiting for him with a disapproving glare. It was after three, and all of the classes had been dismissed for the day. The only people in the building were the people who were there for after school and the people who had an appointment with him.

"Hello?"

Joshua's body tensed when he heard someone call out. Then Kelly's head popped around the corner, and he was relieved.

"I thought you left."

"I did, but I had to set the room up with the task again for the group."

"What does that mean?"

"It means when they left, the Lego car they had to get across the bridge will be gone, and there will be a little remote control car that needs to get across the bridge. The fact that it moves and the different weight will mean they have to think about all the factors tomorrow. I've also changed the budget for their prom night and reduced it by twenty-five percent, and I've given them coupons. It should be interesting to see what they do."

As Kelly spoke about the kids doing their project, he could see her light up with excitement. It made her positively glow.

"Oh, by the way, you had a visitor."

Joshua let his head fall into his hands. "But it's not really a visitor because she lives with me. At least she does for the next week. It was my Aunt Ann, right?"

Kelly nodded. "It was. It looked like she was here to meet you for lunch. Maybe the two of you didn't coordinate well today. Don't worry, it wasn't a problem. I took her to lunch, and she was fine."

Once again, Joshua was so entranced just looking at the way she moved that he almost missed it. "Did you say you went to lunch with Ann?"

"Yes, I did, and it was fine."

"Did she talk about my mother or my brother?"

"Not really. She said in very polite terms that you are a horrible nephew. That you don't make time for her even though she's trying her best to be there for you, but you're inconsiderate."

"Ow! I think I like the way she says it, and I never thought I'd say that."

Kelly smiled. "I do have a way with words."

Joshua smiled back. "And with letters, so I've witnessed."

" It's already forgotten. Group three is back in the main room."

"How many letters did you let them build?"

"Up to J."

"First, let me thank you for taking out my aunt. I want to make sure that you have more material to use in your training sessions. I saw that you already started using some of the things we did at the zoo. I was very impressed. How about tomorrow, I come to pick up my girlfriend, and we go out."

"Is this going to be one of those poor dates again?

If so, I think you should tell me in advance, and I'll see if I can get my parents to give me my allowance."

"As your boyfriend, I have to tell you I have all the cash we need."

Kelly started laughing before he had even finished the sentence.

"I guess that means I better eat before we go out."

Eight

As promised, Joshua showed up on Kelly's front doorstep at nine o'clock the next morning. Unlike the last time, Kelly was prepared. As soon as he rang the doorbell, she opened the door.

In his hand, he had a box fresh from the Sweet Blooms bakery. He had told the waitress to pack it with whatever she thought would make a woman happy. He was interested to see what she packed. He knew today would be a new experience for her, and if it took a box of pastries to get her to go, then so be it.

Today she had dressed in another set of blue jeans and a purple top that said "Top Trainer" on it. It was funny to him; as time went on, he wasn't as enthralled by her beauty but with the things that were so her. Joshua loved the little gap she had between her two front teeth. He also started to notice her little idiosyncrasies. Right before she was about to deliver bad or abrasive news, she took a breath. He didn't know if she was taking it for the person out of pity or for herself while bracing herself. It didn't matter. What mattered was, they were all the things he really liked about Kelly.

"You're here, and you have food," she said. "You thought you needed to bribe me for today?"

"It's supposed to be what a woman would want. And the short answer is yes." He held the box out in front of him. "I have coffee in the truck. All you need to do is get in the truck, so we can go on our date."

Kelly smiled at him. "You're a crafty one, Joshua. Before I sell out, I want a taste and a see. What happens if there's nothing in the box?"

Joshua looked hurt and appalled. "First of all, I would never think to do something like that. And you know what they say, you suspect others of doing the things you would do. It's not my craftiness we should be questioning."

He opened the box, and her eyes went wide.

"Good enough. I'm coming! Let me grab my jacket."

When Kelly got into the truck, Joshua gave her a pastry. They drove for about half an hour. Finally, in the middle of nowhere, Joshua stop the truck. When Kelly got out of the truck, she looked all around. To Kelly, it looked like Joshua had just pulled over on the side of the road.

"Where are we?"

"We're almost there. We just need to go up that path."

Kelly looked at the path that Joshua was pointing to. It was a wide enough path, and it went between two boulders. Just when she was about to protest walking on the path, Joshua came around with the box and the coffee. Joshua took the lead going up the path. About five minutes later, the path opened up, and they were on top of a boulder that overlooked a canyon. They found a nice place to sit, and then Joshua gave Kelly the box of pastries.

"What are we supposed to do up here?" she asked.

"We're supposed to be away from everyone else. We're supposed to dream about what great things we'll do tomorrow."

"Teens have those kinds of thoughts?"

"The first time I came up here was with Jordan."

"How did you get up here? You must have been really young."

Joshua smiled. "We were fourteen going on fifteen years old. According to us, we were almost men," he said with the laughter in his voice.

"It's funny the things that you remember. I remembered coming up here with him. I even remember that we came up on a Saturday. The weather was perfect, and we had "borrowed" the old stick shift truck that dad had. It didn't matter how hard you pushed the gas pedal, that truck wouldn't go any faster than thirty miles an hour. We knew because we tried to get it to go faster all the time."

"It sounds like you and your brother took the truck out to all sorts of places, not just to the place of high contemplation and meditation," she said jokingly.

Joshua stopped and looked around. "Wow, this is the first time I've really said anything about Jordan that wasn't concerning his death."

Kelly was surprised. "I wouldn't have guessed that one. I figured you would always be talking about him because you were twins."

Joshua shook his head. "No, I don't. I think it was too hard for everyone in my family. So we just stopped talking about Jordan. Then, as time went on, we just stopped talking at all."

"I talk about my foster mom all the time. It helps me

to remember all the good she did when she was alive. It also helps me to remember to appreciate everyone while they're here because you just never know."

Kelly looked around and let out a breath. "I think I would have made a horrible teen."

Joshua laughed. "I don't think that's the way it works."

"Okay, since you've done this before, what did you dream about when you were young?"

Joshua smiled. "I dreamed that I would make a lot of money and then I would travel the world over. You?"

Kelly lost her smile and shook her head. "I don't think so."

"Come on, it's about sharing."

"Yeah, that sharing thing. What comes after the sharing thing?"

"It's called trust."

Kelly shook her head.

"I thought we could skip sharing and do the next module, but this might be the easier one."

"Do you remember the dreams you had when you were young?"

"I do. My dreams were about finding a foster home that would keep me, and I did."

"Okay, let's change it up. Tell me about your dreams now that you're an adult."

Kelly looked out across the rocks, and a small smile came across her face.

"I dream about doing something that I think my foster mom would be really proud of."

Joshua gave her a second look. "You don't think your foster mom would be totally thrilled with all the progress and success you've had? You can retire way before the regular age."

Kelly shook her head.

"She was an amazing woman who believed in charity. I think she would be happy that I can support myself, but I'm not so sure she'd be happy that I make people pay for something she gave me for free. The training center, I think, is something she'd be proud of."

Kelly took another bite out of her pastry and then nodded to Joshua that it was his turn.

"Your turn. What do you dream of now that you're a big person?" she laughed.

"I want to build something that I know will help troubled teens. I think the training center will do that for me."

"Well, look at that. We're sharing dreams, and I think that should count for this part of being a teen," Kelly said as she popped in the last of the powered apple crumb cupcake.

"You do realize you ate the whole box."

Kelly smiled. "Yes, I do realize that, and I feel as though you didn't plan appropriately."

"How do you figure?"

"You had a box to get me here, but where is the box to get me back down?"

Both of them laughed until they were on their sides.

Kelly looked around. "It's a great view."

"This used to be part of a science station back in the day. They took the rest but left this platform. A lot of the kids come up here."

He looked at Kelly and saw she had some powder on her face from the cupcake. She caught him smiling at her.

"What is it?"

"You have the evidence on your face." She took a swipe at it, but instead of it going away, she smeared it.

"Stop. Let me."

Joshua reached out and cupped her chin, then used his thumb to brush away the powder. Her smile went away, and she closed her eyes and leaned towards him. He thought of all the reasons this was the worst idea he had ever had. None of them mattered. As his thumb went over her skin, it was a joy unto itself. Then, when he leaned in, and he was right above her lips, he whispered her name.

"Kelly?"

He left the decision to her. For a moment, they were a breath away from one another, and then she gave that slight nod of her head, her eyes closed, and she parted her lips for him.

Joshua would savor this memory forever. This was Kelly in her natural giving state. There were no half measures with Kelly; it was all or nothing, and right now, she was giving it all.

He kissed her, moving slowly across her lips and then to her jaw. Her hands went around his waist, and he repeated the process until he reached her earlobe, and then he heard a soft gasp. That was when his cell phone went off. At first, he thought it was an annoying fly, but as it persisted, he pulled away and pulled his phone from his pocket.

He looked at the caller ID and saw it was Ann.

"Really? Now she decides to call me?"

Kelly laughed. "I think we've got this sharing thing down to a science. I'll see you at the car."

He listened to voice mail she had left.

'Hi Joshua, I'm finally using the phone like you asked me to. I hope I'm not bothering you. You're not picking this up either. See you when you get home.'

Oh no, Aunt Ann, you're not bothering me. You just snatched me out of heaven, but what else is new?

Joshua looked at the proposal that was in front of him for a second time. Today when he had come into work, the principal had given him this new proposal that had been sent from the board. The proposal said that he would be able to get more money for his emergency tree if there were more people who were on the tree and on call.

He had been pacing in his office for the last thirty minutes, looking at this proposal. It was time to take a journey to the coffee machine. Maybe he would be able to make the decision with a little more caffeine.

He went to the teacher's lounge, and there he saw Ethan young talking to the principal. Evan saw him at the coffee machine and left the principal, walking over to him.

"What are you doing here?" Joshua asked.

"I just came out to see how the center was going. Penny told me it was great, and I wanted to let you know. When I walked in the front door, the principal was lying in wait for me. If you hadn't come in, I was going to have to fake a call," Ethan said.

"You have to anticipate that when almost all of the technology and fixes we have in the school are from your donations."

Ethan held his hands up. "It's not me. It's Lydia."

"Well, the checks all have your name on them," Joshua joked.

"Hey, what's wrong? You don't look like your regular, happy self."

"Today, or last night, the principal put a proposal on my desk."

"Okay?"

"He says that I should say the proposal says the school board will give us more money for the emergency tree."

"Sounds good so far," said Ethan.

"The catch is, there has to be more than one person on the tree."

"Ahh, that could be an issue. Who would you pick?"

"Well, that's the other issue. They don't want me to pick; they want it to be the principal. Now they do say that the principal being on the tree will only be a temporary measure, but it will be the case for at least three months."

Both of the men gathered their coffee and walked back to Joshua's office. Evan took a seat in front of Joshua's desk.

" Okay, well, let's start with what's good here."

Joshua nodded. "Having the extra money for the program would be great. And I'm actually looking for some other people to join the emergency tree."

"So it doesn't sound like you disagree with the money. It really sounds like you disagree with the person."

Joshua ran his hands through his hair. "It's not that the principal is a bad person. I just don't know if he is as responsive as he needs to be if he were going to be on the tree."

Evan held out his hands and looked at Joshua. "At the end of the day, you have to do whatever you're going to feel comfortable with and whatever it is that you can live with."

Joshua understood what Ethan was saying. This decision was so important to the emergency tree program. But he didn't want to make the wrong decision and have one of his kids not have the support they need when they need it.

If he were honest, he would say that this program meant a lot to him personally. It was one of those programs that he wished would have been around when he and Jordan were younger.

"We have to go ahead and make these kinds of decisions all the time. We want to go ahead and start a program that is for a good cause. When we start the program, it's small. The smaller it is, the easier it is to manage. But if we want to make a program that will help others and go beyond where we are, we have to take a chance on other people."

"And what do you do when you make a mistake, Ethan?"

Ethan laughed. "Who says that I ever make a mistake?"

Both men laughed at Ethan's joke. "Look, Joshua, there isn't an easy answer, period. The best I can tell you is the same thing I tell myself when I have to make a big decision. I need to decide on the decision that I can live with."

Kelly was suspicious when she received the lunch invitation from Ann Glen. The first thing she said was, "Please don't tell Joshua." They had decided to meet at the same place they met before. Kelly arrived almost ten minutes early because she was so anxious to find out what it was that Ann wanted.

"Hello, Kelly. I want to thank you so much for coming out today."

"I have to tell you I was a little surprised to get the invitation. I was even more surprised that you didn't want me to tell Joshua."

"I know it must all sound so nefarious and shady. But the truth of the matter is that I am at an impasse. I've heard Joshua talk about you in the house, and when he talks about you, his face lights up. Once upon a time, my nephew used to be able to talk to me like that. But things have happened, and now I think the both of us have forgotten that we're family."

"I can't speak for any shine that you might be seeing in Joshua, but what I can tell you is that Joshua and I are good friends."

"I'm not asking for you to tell me any of his secrets. I'm just hoping that you'll be able to give me some advice so that I can at least start talking with my nephew again."

"Well, why don't we start with some basics and then work our way up, okay?" Kelly said.

Ann agreed.

"How are you enjoying being here in Sweet Blooms?" Kelly asked.

"To be honest, I can't stand coming here. I think every time I come here, it's always bad news or something that makes me unhappy." Ann shook her head. "I think if I were honest, it has nothing to do at all with the town. I think the problem is that I know Joshua just doesn't like me. If I didn't come to the town to see my sister, he would never call me. And the only thing we seem to have in common to talk about is my sister. You can see how that would probably be a sore subject."

The waitress came by to take the order, and Kelly ordered for them both. She could see that Ann was trying to blink away the tears after the confession she had just made.

"I want you to know, Ann, that what I think you all really need is to sit down with someone and talk about your problems. But if I had to give you some sidebar advice that has no medical backing to it whatsoever, the first thing I would do is have you and Joshua sit down and talk about the thing that broke you up in the first place."

"I tried to talk to him. I tried for years to talk to him."

Kelly reached her hand across the table and covered Ann's.

"I'm not saying you didn't try to talk to him, but what I am saying is that you've both grown, and I think it's time that someone tries again."

"I thought that when my sister went into the home, he would want to be with me. I thought when his father had passed away, and it was only us, that he would want to be with me. But now I have to force my way into his life for one week out of every year. When does he do anything?

It seems like he would do anything for you. I just want him to want us to be a family again."

"Ann, if you came to me hoping that I had some kind of silver bullet or that I could somehow make Joshua do whatever it is he wanted, I'm so sorry to tell you it's not true. But I'll tell you what my foster mom told me. If you want people to treat you a certain way, you have to make sure you treat them the same way."

"You are a trainer. Help me out."

Kelly's face lit up as soon as Ann said that. "Now this part I can help you with. I think what we should do for the rest of our lunch is something I love doing."

"What's that?" asked Ann.

"It's time to role play."

Nine

Joshua used his elbow to ring the bell to Kelly's place. When she opened it, he held up the bags in each hand.

"In the left hand is Chinese food, and in the right hand are movies."

Kelly leaned against her door and looked at both of his hands before she spoke.

"Please explain to me why I would be happy to see a man with Chinese food and movies at my door. This once again sounds like I have a very poor boyfriend," she said with a smile on her face. She stepped to the side so Joshua could come in.

"You are missing the point. Chinese food is important because it means I spent some money already. Also, we are having Chinese food at your place, which means it's going to be cozy. And the movies are so important because it's going to make this date romantic. True, we could go to the movies, but then everybody else would be there. The true sign of trust in every teen couple relationship is when they can be home alone."

"I feel like we need to re-educate teens on what is really romantic. I happen to think surf and turf at a five-star restaurant is really romantic."

While Kelly was talking, Joshua had already pulled out the Chinese food. He had made sure each one of them had their own set of chopsticks. Then, when it was all laid out, he turned to her and presented it as if it was a Michelin star meal. Then he reached into the other bag and pulled out 5 DVDs.

"Tonight you have a choice of not just one, not two, not three, but five different movies we could watch. What would you like to watch tonight? Would you like to watch romance, romance with a twist, a fairytale romance, a romance that can never happen, or romance where somebody dies?"

By the time he was finished explaining what the selections were, Kelly was on the floor in tears, laughing.

"So is this the time that I tell you that I don't watch romances?" asked Kelly.

Joshua shook his head as if he couldn't believe it, but then he put all of the movies away and pulled out his phone.

"For other boyfriends, this might have been a problem, but because you have the best boyfriend, I have come prepared."

"Really?"

"Yes, I will introduce you to the power of Netflix."

Kelly began laughing again. "This date is getting cheaper and cheaper by the minute."

Joshua laughed with her. "It's my understanding from the kids that one of them buys Netflix, and then you give out passwords, so everyone doesn't have to buy it."

"That's horrible."

Joshua shook his head. "These are the problems of teens today."

"To think when I was a teen, I was worried about finding a job."

It was about two hours later that they had finished eating their Chinese food. Both of them were on the sofa, and Kelly was lying in Joshua's arms as they watched a movie on his phone. After the first thirty minutes, Joshua felt uncomfortable. His arm was getting tired holding his phone between them. The arm that Kelly had her head on was going to sleep, and he was sure that he was getting a cramp in his leg. He wanted to extend his leg, but there was no room. He had already tried flexing his hand to get some of the feelings back in it, but that wasn't helping either. Kelly didn't seem to notice. In fact, she seemed totally engrossed in the action flick that they had found.

"Are you okay, Joshua?"

"Oh yeah, sure, no problem. I just wanna make sure you're comfortable."

Kelly started to giggle. "I have to tell you I would be much more comfortable if you would stop flexing your hand. I mean, it's not like you're going numb or anything."

Joshua stopped and looked at the mischievous glint in her eyes.

"How long have you known?"

"Not long. I wouldn't let you suffer, but I did find it cute you didn't want to move me."

Joshua put the phone down and stamped his foot. When he felt the feeling come back, he flexed his hand, and both were normal again.

"Better?" she asked.

Tonight, her hair was up in a ponytail, and he could imagine her being that mischievous teen.

"So, what's next?"

Instead of giving her an answer, he pulled her to him. When she was laying across his chest, he stopped and gave her the opportunity to move.

He threaded his hands into her hair and guided her the remaining way to his mouth. The kiss was more than the others. This kiss was filled with desire and wanting. It didn't take. It gently asked for entry. It asked for acceptance, and it dared her to answer back. She shifted to get a better angle, and then he wrapped his arms around her and deepened the kiss. Then, with a gentle tug, he separated them. Kelly looked at him, confused.

"I'm leaving."

She rolled off of him and stared at him as he gathered up the garbage and repacked his videos.

"How can you just leave?"

"Because I am keeping my word to you."

"Which word would that be?"

He leaned over and gave her a quick kiss.

"The word that said tonight was about trust. You trusted me to come over and watch movies, and you gave me the gift of a kiss. I'm not going to ruin that trust. Nothing but movies and dinner is what happened between us tonight."

When he had packed up everything, and she walked him to the door, she reached out and grabbed his hand.

"Despite my earlier reaction, thank you, Joshua."

"The pleasure was all mine. Good night, Kelly."

"Thank you so much for meeting with us this morning, Ms. Thomson," said the principal of Castle High.

This morning Kelly had gotten a call from the principal. He wanted to know if she could come into the school today. Kelly asked him if she should go and get Joshua and bring him along, but the principal said had no, that she should hold off, and all would be made clear at the meeting.

"Miss Thompson, we've been looking at your success with the training programs with our children, and we are very pleased."

"Please, call me Kelly. And thank you so much."

Kelly knew something was wrong, but she just couldn't put her finger on it. When she had walked into the principal's office this morning, the principal had been there with two other teachers.

"We thought the way that you handled group three was very effective," said the first teacher who identified herself as Leah.

"I really don't like to do things like that to children or adults, but I do find that sometimes you do need to make an example out of someone so everyone will be able to stay in line."

"As a fellow teacher, we thought your techniques were very helpful, and we saw things that we could use in our classrooms as well," Leah added.

It seemed as though Leah was about to say something else when the principal interrupted and got to the point.

"So, Kelly, I know you must be wondering why we called you this morning. Well, the answer is very simple. Ethan Young told me yesterday that he wanted to make sure we were all settled with who was going to take over the training when you left. Now that doesn't mean that you will be leaving anytime soon, but what it does mean is that we need to be trained."

"The training isn't a problem. I have been working with Joshua the whole time. He is more than capable of going ahead and taking over the training. I will, of course, go over some of the other advanced curriculums with him, but I don't think he'll have a problem."

The principal cleared his throat and then looked at Leah. Leah looked at Kelly, and then she explained.

"The issue is, we don't think that Joshua would be the best fit to be the trainer. We think that a teacher would be more suited to do this role. I'm sure you understand as one teacher to another why we might think training the other teachers at Castle would be a better solution."

Kelly sat back in the chair and looked at everyone in the room. Now she understood why no one wanted her to bring Joshua. They were trying to get her to agree that Joshua wouldn't be the best fit for the training center. Kelly had such great hopes. She had hoped that by being in a small town, they wouldn't be subject to the greedy little mindset that she found in the city.

"So, I'm unclear. Why would I need to train a group of teachers if there is only one teaching spot at the training center?"

The other women in the room nodded and smiled as if they thought Kelly was already on board. The principal then decided to explain.

"Well, what we thought we would do is take the salary that would have gone to the trainer and split it up amongst our teachers. That way any of the teachers could go ahead and take turns being the trainer."

"I want you all to know that I hear your concerns. I think if we are going to keep to the original mission of the training center, splitting up into several trainers isn't going to work. The training center was designed with the idea that there would be one trainer who could keep up with all of the things. I'm sure that all of the teachers here are very talented. But their skills are being used by the high school. The other part of the training center has to do with the children being able to trust the person who is at the center. I think we could all agree that all of the children love and trust Joshua. Besides, Joshua hasn't shown me that he will have any problems at all being the trainer as well as being the guidance counselor. In fact, him been a guidance counselor is going to be an asset to him being the trainer."

Everyone had gone silent in the room. Then Leah spoke up.

"I don't want to be rude, but if no one else will say it, I will. Do we really think that Joshua is qualified to go ahead and be the trainer? The training position is supposed to be filled by a person who is observant and can recognize when a child is thriving emotionally and academically. Do we really think that the person who is known as the twin who survived is that person?"

Kelly waited. She waited for the principal to say something, and she waited for the other teacher to say something. She didn't like the way this meeting had been set up. She didn't like the way they had gone behind Joshua's back. But most of all, she didn't like the way they were speaking about Joshua, because he had given so much and he deserved so much more.

"I think we need to understand what the end goal is, and we need to look forward and not backward. There is no one more qualified than Joshua to train the kids. He has an emotional tie to them, and most of all, he has a track record of reliability. That is a skill you can't teach. When Ethan Young comes to me, I'll tell him that I believe Joshua is the best option. All of you have the right to disagree; that's your prerogative. Now, if you will excuse me, I have groups to run."

Ten

Ann was in the kitchen, waiting for Joshua to come down. She had taken the advice that Kelly had given her and decided to create a neutral ground where the both of them could talk. She was out of options, and this might be her last chance to have a relationship with Joshua.

She had made all of Joshua's favorite foods. Tonight, she had made roast beef with mashed potatoes and gravy. She had also made his favorite dessert; it was a sweet potato pie with marshmallows on the top. She wasn't sure what else she could do in order to make tonight more inviting, but she had decided she wasn't going to take offense at anything that he said. If they were going to survive, they needed to find a way to be able to talk to each other.

She thought she would have to go up and call him again, but just when she was about to go, she heard his footsteps coming into the kitchen. He stopped at the doorway.

Ann took the time to really look at him. He had grown up so much. He was dressed in blue jeans, sneakers, and a white polo shirt with the school logo on it. Sometimes, at night, she wondered if trying to have a relationship with him was worth it. Then she remembered she promised her twin that she'd take care of him if anything happened to her.

"What's the occasion?"

"No occasion. I thought we could eat together, and I thought if I made the things that you liked, you'd be more likely to stay."

She saw him consider his options, and then he sat down. Ann was going to do this by the book. Kelly had told her to just serve the main course and talk about nothing but the weather and whatever happened at his job today. Then, when it was time to serve dessert, they could talk about whatever it was she thought had broken them apart.

She followed those instructions to the letter, and she and Joshua made it through the main course. As she brought out the coffee and sliced up the sweet potato pie, she sat down to do the hard work of trying to fix something that had been broken for a long time.

"Joshua, I know things have been strained between us, but I want to try and make it better."

Joshua looked up from his pie and stared her straight in the eye. His gaze never wavered, and then he began to speak.

"Do you really want to talk about this, Aunt Ann?"

Ann gave a shrill laugh. "To be honest, I don't, but I don't want to lose the only family I have, either. So I'm willing to give this a try."

Joshua put down his fork.

"Why do you always call her my mother?"

Ann was expecting some question about Jordan, but this question was out of left field.

"What does that have to do with anything? I thought we were going to talk about things to make our relationship better."

"We are. Can you answer the question?"

Anger and hurt welled up in Ann. She could feel the burning behind her eyes, and she was helpless to control it.

"Is it because you blamed her for Jordan's death?"

Ann was pulled out of her pain when she heard Joshua's voice.

"No, I never blamed her."

Joshua nodded. "I wasn't sure if you did. For a long time, I thought that was why you didn't call her your sister anymore. I blamed myself for a long time for Jordan's death, and then when you stopped calling mom your sister, I thought—"

Ann got up and went to kneel in front of Joshua. This time she let the tears flow. "I'll tell you because you of all people will understand. The day Jordan died, I lost my twin."

Joshua looked confused.

"You can't imagine the grief that a person can feel when someone you love dies. Whatever you can imagine, multiply it by a hundred when it's your child. Patricia was so filled with grief, she shut everyone out. I knew she would shut you out, and your father. But when she shut me out, it was as if I had lost a part of myself. I lost a nephew, and I lost the better half of me."

Ann stood up and wiped her face. She looked up to the heavens. And then she shook her head.

"I was a fool to think I could do this."

Joshua stood and reached for her, but she took a step back.

"It's funny. I thought this evening would end in a different way. I guess I didn't really know what the problem was until we started talking. Or why I picked on you all the time. You see, Joshua, you have some closure because Jordan is gone. It's over. You have the pain to get by, but we all do. I have no closure. My twin is alive, but I can't reach her. The only thing I can do is wait, hope, and pray that one day she'll come back to me or one of us will pass.

"Auntie Ann, I—"

Ann avoided his touch and walked out of the kitchen and to her bedroom.

She thought she knew what the problem was. She thought she could fix it, but all along the problem hadn't been Joshua; it had been her.

"It was so sad, and I had no idea what to do," Joshua said as he finished telling Kelly what happened the night before.

"Joshua, I have to tell you I was the one who told her to talk to you. I really thought it would help," Kelly confessed.

"It did. I'm just not sure where either one of us wants to go from here."

Joshua had shown up on Kelly's front doorstep this morning. As soon as she opened the door, he grabbed her and gave her a kiss.

"Well, good morning to you too. And what did I do to warrant you showing up again, if I see correctly, with another box of Sweet Blooms café sweets?"

"It's just because you are you."

Afterward, they wound up on her couch with coffee and the sweet box.

"Well, at least I know why she was so picky when it came to me."

Kelly stroked Joshua's hair as he lay on her lap, and she popped another pastry in her mouth.

"I think it's great you talked." Kelly took another bite of the pastry and savored the apple on her tongue. When she opened her eyes, Joshua was looking at her with a smile on his face.

"Where do you put it?" he joked.

"It takes a lot of brain power to be a trainer. When you look at these pastries, you should see curriculums. It must take at least three cupcakes for me to make a new curriculum."

Joshua laughed. "I can't say I've ever heard of a person equating their food intake with curriculums."

"You've been deprived," she joked. Thinking about curriculums, she was reminded about yesterday. She needed to tell him about the meeting. She knew he was friends of a sort with the principal and didn't want to cause him any unwarranted stress at his job. Just when she was about to bring it up, he spoke.

"Did I tell you about the funding that the principal got for the emergency tree?"

"No, but it sounds great. I think that is a service the school really needs, and you can hire some people if you get funding."

"The money comes with the caveat that the principal needs to man the emergency tree with me for three months, but I'm not sure that the principal is the one."

Kelly heard his words, and she knew this was not the time to tell him that the principal was trying to kick him out of his job at the training center.

"It sounds like you are really concerned."

"I am. I don't want to make a mistake with the kids."

"Well, my thought is just what my foster mom would say."

"And that is?"

"To make a decision, you should look yourself in the mirror and say the decision out loud. If you can do it and still look yourself in the eye, then it's a good decision."

"I'll have to take that into consideration. So, how have you liked living the life of a couple."

Kelly put her hand to her forehead and then said in a dramatic voice, "It's so hard to fend off the other people, but because we're in a relationship, I'm willing to do it for you."

Joshua sat up. "You know, through this whole ordeal I've never asked you if you'd ever been in a relationship where you thought about marriage."

Kelly smiled at him. "Once. It was a mistake, obviously, and I was very young."

Joshua rolled his hands to encourage her to tell. "I was on the job, and I thought we were on the same page. But we weren't. He thought he would marry an asset to his company, and I thought he cared about me."

"Ah, now it all makes sense about the rules."

"And you, Prince Charming?" she asked.

"No, not ever. I think I was so tied up with the kids or school, there just wasn't time."

"My foster mother would say, 'You make time for those things.'"

"She'd be right. So, I have to ask, when you were in the other relationship, and you knew it was going south, were you ever tempted to stray?" Joshua asked.

"The word stray sounds so much better than cheat. The answer to your question would be no. Even when I knew the relationship was over, I still didn't think I could even date until we had officially broken everything off."

Joshua looked away from her and then shrugged. "You know, Kelly, you are an attractive woman. And no one would blame you if you were ending our relationship and starting another. The other thing is, because you are attractive, I would assume you get a lot of offers."

Kelly turned Joshua's face so he could look her in the eye. "Being attractive doesn't give anyone the right to cheat on another person. Being attractive doesn't mean you can betray someone's trust, either. If you love somebody, then you have to love them all the way. You are the only one I'm seeing, just in case you needed me to make it plain."

"I'm asking because we are in a unique situation. I mean, how many times have you heard a guy say, 'Hey, let's pretend to be a couple so you can be able to do your job better,'" Joshua joked.

"I hear you, and I want you to know I'm with you until the end."

Joshua smiled "Well, I think that we have covered the basics of being a teen, and we should celebrate our trust milestone by going out on an adult outing."

Kelly clapped her hands.

"Are we going to a real restaurant?"

Joshua looked at her and said, "No, still not going to one of those."

"Well, then, whatever. I probably won't even notice. When is this adult moment supposed to happen."

"I'm thinking tomorrow is a good time for the event. It will be our first adult date."

<h1 style="text-align:center">Eleven</h1>

Kelly couldn't explain it, but she was looking forward to her first real adult date with Joshua. She put on a blue sundress and matching sandals. When he told her to meet him at the park, she didn't question it. When she saw him with the picnic basket, she was absolutely thrilled. Joshua was dressed in blue jeans that hugged his lean legs and a white polo top that outlined his shoulders and hugged his lean abs.

"Your basket looks impressive. It looks like you had a plan or something," she joked.

"It's not the five-star establishments you are used to, but I'm told the very best deli sandwiches which can be bought in Sweet Blooms are in here. And in case you decide that deli sandwiches aren't what you are in the mood for, I also have six cupcakes from the Sweet Blooms Café."

"How could I possibly resist with a basket like that?"

They found a picnic table underneath a large tree. Joshua began to unpack the picnic basket. He took out a sandwich and gave one to Kelly and then gave one to himself. She was amazed by how well packed the basket was. She wanted to make sure to ask him where he had gotten it done so they could do this again.

"I imagine this must be your first picnic with a date," Joshua said.

"Really? Well, it's not my first picnic, but it is my first picnic that a date has taken me on."

"In my head, I see you dating muscle guys."

"Muscle guys?"

"You know, the guys who go to the gym all the time?"

"Ah, I don't call them muscle guys though," she said, laughing.

"What do you do you call them?"

"No necks," she whispered. When Joshua heard her, he nodded his head and started to laugh.

"And to set the record straight, I've only been out with one no neck, and it was too distracting for me to go out with him again."

"Yes, Kelly, that was the thing I noticed first about you. You always say exactly what's on your mind. I never have to wonder if there is something left unsaid or if you're holding back."

"Whatever. You say that now, but I'm pretty sure the first thing you noticed about me was my face."

For once, Kelly was having fun. Here she was in the middle of a small town, and she was with a man who allowed her to be her. Everything was perfect at this moment. The sun was up, there wasn't too much wind, and the park wasn't crowded. It wasn't a four-star or five-star restaurant; it was better than that.

Kelly had never been with someone with whom she felt so free. Being with Joshua was like being with her best friend and her life partner all at the same time.

There was nothing that she couldn't talk about, and there was nothing that was forbidden to talk about. She could say what she really wanted to say without the fear of being judged.

Then, just as quickly as it came, the moment was stolen away by a dark shadow that fell across to picnic table.

"Hello, Kelly."

Kelly looked at the end of the table, and standing there with a smirk on her face was Leah, the teacher from Castle High. Leah's hair was pulled back into a ponytail, and Kelly thought it did her face a disservice. The ponytail appeared to be so tight that it pulled Leah's eyes back and up.

"Hello, Leah. How are you?"

Joshua looked at Kelly with a confused look on his face.

"I didn't know the two of you knew each other," Joshua said. "Leah, did you want to join us?"

Leah looked at Joshua and shook her head. "I'm surprised at you, Joshua Case."

Kelly saw Leah getting ready to wind up. An errant wind came by, and Kelly wished it had been a gale of epic proportions to stop the chaos she knew Leah was about to deliver. She knew this was going to put a damper on the picnic, but it was probably best that Joshua knew about the people he worked with.

"Joshua, I don't think Leah wants to join us at all."

Joshua looked between Kelly and Leah and knew something was off, but he couldn't tell what it was.

"Kelly, what is it?"

When Leah heard him call her Kelly, she jumped on it.

"Is that how it works now? So you're calling her Kelly now, and you're taking her out in public to go on a date."

Joshua was still confused. "Leah, why are you so angry?"

"Didn't she tell you?"

"Leah, I think you should leave this alone. I didn't say anything because I was asked not to," Kelly replied.

"Well, anything that was said at the meeting should be said now. You are just passing through Sweet Blooms; you don't have to stay the rest of your life here. At the end of the day, Joshua is one of us unless that's changed too."

Joshua stood up and put his hands out to stop everyone from talking.

"It seems like everyone knows what the conversation is about except me."

Kelly saw Leah take a seat, and for a moment she wanted to push the picnic table over so Leah would tumble to the ground. Kelly thought about jumping in front of Leah and telling Joshua she would explain, but pride kept her in place. This was just one more time when people would say something about her, and people would either give her a chance or they wouldn't. She wasn't worried, though. She knew Joshua would wait to hear her side.

"Well, you know, Joshua, how the principal has been trying to find new ways to give us a raise. We called in your Kelly and asked her to train us so we could make some more money. We told her that if she trained us, we could help out at the training center. She said no. Then we asked her if it was a matter of us teaching or you teaching, and she said she wouldn't even try to teach us. That she was going to recommend to Ethan that she couldn't train any of us and that she could only train one person."

Joshua looked at Kelly, and she expected to see him laughing at the story. Instead, what she saw made her take a step back. Gone was the man she thought she could trust. In his place was a man who was a stranger to her.

She said she wouldn't, but she couldn't stop the words from coming out of her mouth.

"Joshua?" Kelly said.

Leah interrupted with her question. "Go ahead, Joshua, ask her if we had the meeting."

Joshua turned to Kelly, and she could see she was already guilty in his eyes. She didn't wait for him to ask. She answered it.

"Yes, I was at the meeting, and yes, the meeting happened."

"You see, you see," Leah parroted.

"Leah, I want you to listen to me. I want to thank you for telling me about the meeting, but I can assure you that Kelly didn't have any malicious thoughts in her head about taking money away from the teachers. She might not have understood the problems that the teachers have, but she wouldn't block someone from getting money."

"Joshua, how can you—"

"I know Kelly's work ethic, and she wouldn't do that."

For a moment, Kelly thought that Joshua was on her side. But then she heard him say that he knew her work ethic. He didn't say he knew her. She waited while Joshua calmed Leah down. It must have been about ten minutes later before he was able to get Leah settled.

While she had been there, Leah had said everything from thinking Kelly wanted to get the teachers fired to mentioning a rumor going around that Joshua was spending time with Kelly to make sure he got the job. Leah had said that was going around because why else would Kelly be spending time with Joshua?

After Leah left, Joshua didn't say a thing. He just started to pack up the picnic.

"You're not going to ask me anything?" she whispered.

"No, there isn't a need."

Those words hurt more than if he had yelled at her. Anger came on the heels of hurt.

"Is that all it takes? One of your friends says something, and that's it?"

Joshua never stopped packing. When he was done, he looked at her and asked, "What did you say? Being attractive doesn't give anyone the right to betray another's trust."

"I didn't betray you!" she said through clenched teeth.

"Did you go to the meeting?"

"Yes, I did."

"Did you tell me? It was about the training center. You know how much the center means to me and why. What would you call it if I hid information away from you about the training center?"

"That's what this is about, the training center. It's not about me. It's about you making sure you can work out your guilt at the training center. It's about making sure people don't think I'm helping you out."

Joshua didn't deny it, and Kelly backed away. She had thrown the words out to make him fight and deny them, and even those were turning out to be true.

"Maybe this is for the best. It turns out that neither one of us may know the other as well as we thought."

Kelly backed up, and Joshua called out. She stopped thinking maybe he would try to fix it.

"I can take you home."

She heard the words, but she pulled her shoulders back and buried her heart deep.

"I can get myself home. I have enough cash to do that. So thank you, but no thanks." She turned and walked away; she didn't know where she was going except for the fact that it was away from Joshua.

Twelve

Joshua realized it was time to go back to the barbershop. After the last couple of days and all that he had been through with finding out that Kelly had betrayed him, he figured going to the barbershop would be a safe place for him.

He stood outside the door and heard the familiar sounds of men talking. He opened the door, expecting to be greeted by the familiar calls from the guys. Instead, as soon as he stepped into the shop, everyone went silent. It was so noticeable that Joshua had to look behind himself to see if there was a woman behind him.

Finally, Mr. Harold spoke.

"Come on in, boy. We all need to talk to you." Whatever it was, Joshua knew this wasn't going to be good. As he walked into the shop, the men either gave him a nod or shook their heads as he passed by.

"So it seems that you and the girl named Kelly are having a disagreement. Is that true?"

"No, Mister Harold, we are not having a disagreement. To have a disagreement, we would have to be talking to each other."

After he made that statement, the room went quiet for about five seconds, and then all of the men in the barbershop started to laugh. They patted themselves on the back, and one or two of them even wiped their brow before looking at him. When Joshua looked at Mr. Harold, even he was smiling.

"I am so confused," Joshua said.

Davy's father just waved him on to take a seat as he spoke to him. "You're not confused. You're just young and dumb, but don't worry; we are here to help you."

The shop started to go back to normal noise level, and all Joshua could do was sit in the chair and wait for someone to explain things.

Mr. Harold decided to take the lead.

"So this is what happened, Joshua. It turns out that your Kelly had an argument with Leah."

"She's not my Kelly," he said in a low voice.

Mr. Harold just ignored him. "Anyway, your Kelly got into some kind of hubbub with Leah. If you look over there, that's Leah's husband. Well, Leah said that your Kelly is taking advantage of you and stopping everyone from getting some extra money."

Joshua listened to Mr. Harrold and couldn't believe how what he thought was a simple moment in the park was turning into the talk of the town.

"Now, if the teachers can't make extra money because of your Kelly—"

Joshua took in a deep breath and let it out. "She's not my Kelly."

"Uh-huh. Like I was saying, it turned out that Sally's momma knows Davy's momma and they told Davy's dad. He's the third one in the line that said Leah was wrong. Well, by the time they were done, all the women who agreed with Leah wouldn't talk to all the women who didn't agree with Sally. Now they won't talk to each other in the street, and the only place the men can gather that is approved by all the women is this shop. And I have to tell you, half the men here ain't even here for a cut!"

Joshua looked around, and every one of the men was nodding in agreeance with Mr. Harold.

"You all don't understand. She didn't tell me the truth."

Davy's dad spoke up. "I think it's just easier to forgive her, and then you all can go back and fix the problem at the school."

Joshua looked around. "Is that what this is all about to everyone? Do you want me to fix the problem at the training center?" Joshua asked.

"Now, Joshua, I need you to think about what you are doing. I know you think you're right but—"

Joshua looked at Mr. Harold. "You all haven't even heard what I have to say."

Mr. Harold folded his cape and called the next man to sit in the chair.

"No, Joshua, you haven't heard what we've been saying in this shop for years. We can't think of one thing that any of our wives would do that we would want them to be unhappy about for any amount of time. In the end, it doesn't matter who was wrong and who was right. As long as you can talk it through, you'll be fine."

Joshua heard them and saw all of the nodding heads, and it made sense until he thought about what Kelly had said to him, and then he thought different. He didn't answer Mr. Harold; instead, he just went home. He needed to think, and he couldn't do that at the shop.

Joshua was no closer to a conclusion the next morning than he was the night before. When he went to work, he decided he was going to do the only thing he could. He watched Kelly say goodbye to the class in the training room and then he called her name.

"Kelly?"

She turned around, and instead of seeing her smile, her face was blank.

"What can I do for you, Joshua?"

Had he ever heard her sound so cold? This woman was driving him crazy, and he had to cut the ties; otherwise, it was going to drive him crazy.

"Can I talk to you after work?"

"I'll be at my car in ten minutes. I'll wait for you for five minutes if you want to say something." With that, she turned and walked away.

Joshua put some files in his briefcase to review. He knew what he had to say to Kelly; he was just stalling. He was stalling cutting all ties with a woman who couldn't be honest with him. It made no sense. The only thing that made sense was for him to back away from the situation.

When he got to the parking lot, she was in her car, and the engine was running. He looked around to make sure no one else was there.

"I wanted to say thank you for all the work you did showing me the curriculum."

"It was my pleasure. I'm always happy to help someone who wants to learn."

Joshua looked at her and thought, *could she be any colder?*

"Yes, well, it seems like the problem is me teaching at the center, so I've decided that I won't be the teacher."

"Really? I didn't think you'd be swayed by the masses."

"I'm not being swayed by the masses. I'm just saying I have the emergency tree, and Leah was right; the teachers have been trying to get some extra money, so it might work out for everyone."

Kelly nodded as he spoke. "Well, good luck with that."

Joshua was frustrated and angry at her attitude. "Is that it?"

"Is what it, Joshua?"

"I thought… I don't know what I thought."

Kelly turned off her car and got out. "Yes, it's very clear that you didn't know what you thought. What would you like me to do now, Joshua? I'm afraid I don't know how these small town games work."

Joshua tried to breathe through it, but no matter where he turned, he was wrong. "What do you want, Kelly?"

"You know what I want now, Joshua? Nothing! Let me tell you what I wanted before. I wanted a person who was going to listen to me before they decided I was wrong. I wanted someone who would be there and support me. I wanted to be with a man who wanted to go the distance.

"I know, I know, I'm the one who said I didn't want to mix business and personal. But I was wrong.

Somewhere along the line, I thought you were going to be that someone special. It turned out that I was wrong.

"It turned out that you were just like everybody else. So you want to know what I want now? I don't want anything from you, Joshua. Because everything beautiful we had has been thrown away, and you didn't even think it was worth hearing me out before you made your decision."

With those words, she got into her car and drove off. Joshua watched her leave, and he had a sinking feeling that he had missed something.

"Hey, Joshua" Joshua turned towards the sound of his name and saw the principal coming towards him.

"I'm glad I finally caught up to you. Do you have time for some coffee?" Joshua said yes, and they talked for the next two hours.

Two and a half hours later, Joshua walked into his home. After talking with the principal, he realized he had made the biggest mistake of his life, not listening to Kelly. What could he say to her? What would she even listen to now? There was no one for him to blame, except himself. Kelly had been right. The guys in the barbershop had been right.

Even more importantly, now, it was time for Joshua to take a serious look at how he had been handling Jordan's death. After talking with his aunt, and after their dinner conversation, he had to come to some of his own realizations. Kelly was right. He was trying to make it through survivor's guilt. The training center was going to be his new way of trying to make up for being alive.

If he was really honest with himself, Joshua would have to admit that what he needed right now was definite help. He hadn't accepted the therapist's help before because he didn't want anyone to know that he had a problem. Now he needed help more than anything else. He needed someone who could help him deal with Jordan's death.

He sat in his living room and went over everything that he needed to do. The problem was, he still didn't know how he was going to make it up to Kelly. He didn't know if she would even take him back. He sat in his oversized chair in his living room, leaning his head on the backrest, hoping that an answer would finally come.

He heard Ann's footsteps as she came down the steps. They hadn't been talking to each other ever since he broke up with Kelly. Now that he knew the truth, he realized he deserved every cold shoulder she had been giving him for the last couple of days.

"Ann?"

"Yes, Joshua?"

"I need help."

Ann was in her robe and fluffy slippers. She stopped and peeked at him in the living room.

"Have you found your sense yet?"

Joshua moaned. "I have, and I realize that I have made a huge mess of things."

He heard his aunt let out a deep sigh. "I'm so glad that you've finally come around. Don't worry. I know that Kelly is the sweetest person ever, and if you just throw yourself at her feet, she'll take you back," Ann said with a large smile.

"This throwing myself at her feet thing. I feel like you think this should be a public moment."

"It should be if it's sincere," Ann chimed back.

Joshua rested against the headrest. When did life get so complicated, and how could he have messed up so bad?

Joshua got up from his chair, and he started to go upstairs. The good news was, he knew the truth. The bad news was, he didn't have a plan to fix what he had already broken.

Thirteen

Kelly didn't like to lose. It's true; the reason she was unhappy was because Joshua was just too blind and narrow-minded to see beyond his pain. When she had met him in the parking lot, the first thing she thought was he had finally come to his senses. But then, after he said he didn't want to be a trainer anymore, she knew that he had let his pain dull any common sense he had.

What made her so angry was that he wasn't willing to fight. He wasn't willing to fight for them. So what started out as a deep hole and an abyss of pain that she thought she would never recover from began to transform into anger. Anger she knew how to deal with. Anger didn't hurt so bad.

Three days later, her anger was gone. If she didn't know any better, she'd think that Joshua had been avoiding her altogether. She knew she was right. But being right didn't fix anything. She wanted it to be like the movies; she wanted to be right, and she wanted to get the guy.

Kelly always believed in telling herself the truth. Her foster mom had always told her that. You can tell the world whatever it is you want, but when you go home, make sure you're telling the woman in the mirror the truth.

The truth was, she couldn't go on like this. She didn't need to. She would look at the project tomorrow and tie things up. It wasn't healthy for her to stay around, waiting for him to come to his senses. And if he did come to his senses, would she want to take him back?

No, Kelly knew it was time for her to go. If she went to him and explained everything, they might get back together, but then she would have to worry about what would happen the next time someone went to him. Would it always be she'd have to explain everything? No, the time had come. She would give a call to Ethan in the morning and let everybody know she was wrapping up and handing in all of her closing documents.

It was time for Kelly to look out for herself, even if it was going to be one of the most painful things she had to do. It was time to move on.

Joshua was miserable. He had made a mistake, and everybody knew it. When he came into work, all the teachers would give him looks of disapproval. He knew that the students knew something was wrong too. Joshua had come into his office just the other day, and someone had left a book on his desk that was titled *Men Are from Mars, Women Are from Venus*. Attached was a little sticky note saying 'hope his helps.' Things were so bad that when he went to the shop, the guys would just shake their heads as he went by.

The problem was, he didn't know how to fix it. He didn't have a clue on what to do. Every day he tried to think of the words he needed to say to Kelly, but all of them seemed foolish. When he tried to talk to his aunt, she would just look at him and shake her head. The only words she had for him these days were 'pride goeth before the fall.'

He loved Kelly, and he knew he had made a mistake. Just as Joshua sat down at his desk to try and drown himself in his work, the phone rang.

"Hello?"

"Hey, Joshua, it's me, Ethan. I just wanted to give you a heads up. Kelly says she thinks we're good, and she's going to do a knowledge transfer before she leaves. So, however you all want to do that make sure the right people are in the room is fine with me."

"Yeah, no problem."

"Good. I knew I could count on you."

When he hung up the phone, the first thing that hit him was a sense of loss that he hadn't felt since Jordan died. How could she leave? Then, when he thought about the last couple of days, he had to ask himself how could she not?

He pushed away from the desk. It was time to settle this once and for all. His mind was still a blank as he left his office. He had no idea what he was going to say to Kelly. The only thing he did know was he had to try whatever it took and give it his all before he let the best thing he'd ever had in his life walk out. For once, Joshua was prepared to give it his all, no matter the outcome.

All of the words he had been telling himself sounded really good as he was walking down the hall. But now that he was in front of her door and looking inside, all of those words went away. In fact, all of those good intentions seemed to be fading by the second.

As he looked through the window of the classroom, he could see that she was once again giving the teams a creative problem to solve. He saw the students all standing around their versions of bridges, totally engrossed in the lesson. She had a way of doing that, of making people come together.

He thought about coming back later. And then remembered there would be no later. It was now or never. Not knowing exactly what he was going to do, he opened the door.

"Yes?"

Joshua stepped into the classroom, and all of the eyes fell on him.

"Can I talk to you for a minute?" he asked.

Kelly looked around the room and then looked back at him. "I'm sorry, Mr. Case, I'm busy at the moment."

The was a collective groan that went through the room, and he even heard someone say, "So sorry man."

He looked around the class, and he shrugged.

"Okay, I don't need you to leave. We can discuss this right here."

He saw the look of shock on her face. "Mr. Case—"

Joshua went in front of the class, and he wrote the words extra credit on the board. He looked at the students and began.

"So today, everyone in the class will have the opportunity to earn some extra credit. All you need to do is participate. We may not be able to find an answer, but we have to try."

Everyone in the class nodded and waited for him to continue. Sally was in the class, and she smiled.

"What's the problem?"

"My girlfriend and I are having a disagreement, and now she wants to break up with me. It's so bad that she won't even talk to me anymore."

He watched Kelly's mouth open like a fish out of water. When one of the students giggled, she closed her mouth and crossed her hands over her chest.

One of the boys asked, "Did you do something wrong?"

Sally turned towards him. "Of course he did something wrong!"

The boy looked at Sally. "How can you know he did anything? He didn't say."

Sally looked to the heavens as if she needed to find some patience to explain the situation. "He already said they are having a disagreement, but if she's not talking to him, they're not having a disagreement; they're having a fight and he doesn't know it, so he's wrong."

Joshua looked at Sally, and what he'd thought was a good idea no longer seemed that way all of a sudden. He wondered if he should have thought on it longer. Then Sally turned to him.

"Well, Mr. C, this is what I think you should do. I think you need to go ahead and buy her something you know she really likes. Then go to her home and beg her forgiveness, and maybe after a couple of days of begging, she'll take you back."

One of the boys again chimed in. "Why does he have to do the begging? Why can't she say sorry first."

Sally gave him a long look and shook her head. "My mom says it's always the bigger person who apologizes first. She says that if you really love someone, you won't let a misunderstanding get between you two."

Joshua looked at Kelly while Sally was speaking.

"To think I wasted the past few days trying to figure out what to do. It looks like I should have just come into this room earlier and put the both of us out of our misery."

"What are you saying, Joshua?"

"I'm saying I want another chance. I'm saying, Kelley Thompson, will you please go out on a date with me? I promise it'll be a real adult date. We may even make it to a real restaurant."

Kelly nodded. "You hurt me."

"I was scared, and sometimes the truth hurts."

Kelly shook her head, and Joshua held his hand up.

"Give me a day before you answer. After a day of you thinking about it, if you decide no, I'll accept that."

Kelly looked at him strangely. "A day?"

"Yes, but my day starts tomorrow morning."

Kelly nodded. "Okay, you've got a day."

The class cheered. "Woohoo! Go and get ready." As he left the classroom, the kids cheered him on with encouraging phrases "You can do it."

Kelly shook her head, smiling at them all. He wasn't out of the woods, but at least he had her smiling.

Ann hoped the sun being up was a good sign of the meeting to come. She had finally gone to visit her sister. She took a deep breath. Patricia was her sister. Every year, she had been coming to visit her sister at this home, and every year, she left more discouraged than when she had originally arrived. After talking with Joshua, she was now ready to finally face her sister.

She realized now they had never really talked about Jordan's death. It was time to begin the healing process.

Ann had always loved coming to these apartments. When she and Patricia were kids, they had decided that they would both retire to the same place. When Ann had first visited these apartments, it was just like they had talked about as children. The grounds were well manicured and clean. Everywhere you looked, there were flowers, and the residents could be seen coming and going. The staff was always smiling and were very helpful. But most of all, the thing that really caught Ann's attention was that the colors in the apartments were always bright.

The nurse said that Patricia with outside today. Ann walked through the inner courtyard, and sitting on a bench by herself was her twin, Patricia. She didn't say anything to Patricia as she sat down next to her. She didn't say anything to her because it used to be they never had to say anything to each other When the other one needed something, or when they wanted to talk, the other one just knew.

"Hi, Patricia. I wanted to talk to you about Joshua. A couple of nights ago, Joshua and I had dinner. I know it doesn't sound like much. What you have to know is, I haven't been able to keep in touch with Joshua like I said I would. After Jordan, everything changed.

When you came here, I was all alone. I missed you, Patricia. I missed you so much. I couldn't be there for Joshua. I know when we were growing up, we said we'd look after each other's children. But I couldn't do it without you, Patricia.

"Pat, you haven't spoken to me in so long I've almost forgotten the sound of your voice. I don't know if any of this matter to you anymore, but I wanted to tell you. Remember, we don't have secrets between us, right?"

Ann looked next to her to see if Patricia had moved at all while she was talking. But like every year, there was no acknowledgment from Patricia. She just sat there looking forward. Ann let out a sigh of regret. Then, like she did every year, Ann put her hand on the bench in between her and Patricia. She put her hand out far enough so that Patricia could reach it if she wanted to. Like every year, she waited. She waited and hoped that she'd get some sort of response from Patricia.

Just when she was about to say her goodbyes, Ann felt a warm, frail hand on top of hers. Ann looked over to see Patricia looking back at her with tears in her eyes. Patricia didn't speak; she just patted Ann's hand and then held onto it.

Ann sniffed back the tears of joy and nodded. Then Patricia looked away but still held Ann's hand. Ann looked forward too. It wasn't everything, but this, at least, was a start.

Fourteen

Joshua had left the school right away; he had a woman to win. All he could think about was what he could do to show her how much he really cared about her. Plans and ideas rolled through his head as he drove his truck to the front of his home.

That was when he saw someone sitting on the steps in front of his house. There wasn't anything unusual about coming home and finding one of the kids on his steps, but he had a bad feeling about this one because school was still in session.

When he got out of his truck, he was able to see that it was Davy. As he got closer, he didn't like the way that Davy was standing. And by the time he was almost to the steps, he could see that Davy wasn't well.

Davy was standing by the time Joshua got to the steps. Joshua looked at the boy and could tell he had some bruises on his face, and he was holding the side of his rib cage.

"Mr. Case?"

"Davy, what happened?"

There were tears on his face. He tried to wipe them away with the hand that wasn't holding his ribcage.

"I tried to call you," he said in a wobbly voice. Joshua was confused, and then it became clear. He tapped his side pocket and realized the emergency tree phone wasn't with him; it was at the school. The new schedule was, the phone would stay at the school in the daytime, and after school, it would be with Joshua. But someone was always supposed to have the phone on their body.

"Come inside, Davy. Let me look at you, and then we'll go from there."

"Some boys followed me, and I didn't have anywhere to go. So I called while I was walking away from them. No one answered, and they took my money and roughed me up," Davy said in a small voice.

Joshua didn't know what else to do. He was happy that Davy went into the house with him. At least he hadn't lost the boy's trust yet. But this was just what he feared. Just when he thought everything was going well, this happened.

Joshua settled Davy down and then called the emergency line. No one picked up. As each ring passed, his guilt got heavier and heavier. He then placed the call he was dreading to Principal Potts.

"Hello," Potts answered.

"Dorian, it's me, Joshua."

"Oh, Joshua, I heard you are making quite a stir in Ms. Thomson's class."

"Yeah, I guess so. I needed to talk to you, Dorian. I came home and found one of my students on my steps. He has been beaten up."

"No! Is there anything I can do?"

"Dorian, the reason I'm calling is that he said he called the emergency tree, and no one answered."

"Really? I find that hard to believe—"

"Dorian, I just called the line, and no one answered."

"Hold on, let me get the phone." Joshua listened to Dorian rustling for the phone. Finally, he came back to the phone.

"Ah, I see you're correct. I don't know how that happened."

Joshua was trying to hold on to his patience.

"I thought we all agreed we would always have the phone on at all times."

"Well, I'm sure you can understand how that's really not going to be feasible for me at the school. I understand we need to share the responsibility of the phone, but you have to understand that we also need to run a school."

"Dorian, I guess I just don't understand. I thought we had discussed the phone before we decided to take the money from the community board."

"Joshua, I'm going to have to be very honest with you. I understand how much this program means to you, but you gave us this program and didn't give us any training to go with it."

Joshua stuttered. "I thought—"

Principal Dorian interrupted. "I think that's the problem right there, Joshua. You know I really respect you and that we all look up to you in the school. You know what's going on with our children, and we can see that you genuinely care about them. But the emergency tree is bigger than any one of us. It's one of those things that we all need to own if we want it to grow.

"I understand that you started it, and I want you to know that so many of the children have come back and said that they've used the tree, and that it's important to them. But at some point, Joshua, I think you need to let us help you do this. Did I think there were going to be some mistakes made? Yes. Do I wish that they hadn't happened? Again, yes, but we're human. So I think it comes down to you. Help us get better to help the kids or take the tree back."

After Joshua got off of the phone with the principal, he went to check on Davy. When he was sure he was okay, he took Davy home. It was true, Joshua had been holding on to everything for too long. Hearing all of the things that he was doing for his kids was just another way to try to make up for not being able to save Jordan. But now he realized that by trying to control everything, he was hurting the kids he was trying to help. It was time to change.

When he got home, Aunt Ann hadn't returned yet. He checked the messages on his phone and found that the therapist he had reached out to had an opening for him in two weeks. This was another part of the change he was embracing.

He was anxious for Ann to come back here. He knew that she had gone to see his mother at her apartment, and he wanted to know how that went. A few minutes later, the door opened, and in came Aunt Ann.

"Oh, Joshua, I am so happy that you are here. Today was an amazing day. I think I made some decisions that I really needed to."

Joshua looked at how happy Aunt Ann looked. He wasn't sure what had happened, but whatever it was, he could tell it had made her happy.

"I can agree; today has been a rollercoaster day."

The both of them went and sat side by side on the couch. Ann reached out and grabbed Joshua's hand.

"Today, my sister touched my hand."

Joshua smile and then pulled his aunt into his embrace.

"I'm so happy for you, auntie. I know you have been waiting for this for a long time."

"It's a small step, but it's a step nonetheless. I wanted to ask you a question."

"Go ahead."

"Would you mind if I came down here more often? I know that you're a bachelor and that you live alone, and you probably have your own way of doing things, but I feel like I'm just starting to break through and find my sister again. I don't want to lose any more ground."

"I hope you know you don't even have to ask. Lately, I have been surrounded by women who are reminding me of what's important in my life."

After pulling herself together and wiping off tears of happiness, she asked him, "So, did anything exciting happen today?"

Joshua used the next hour to tell her everything that had happened today. Then he and his aunt took the next two hours to plan what he was going to do to keep Kelly after tomorrow.

Kelly waited all day long. She constantly checked her texts, and she hoped that maybe she had received an email from Joshua. Despite everything that happened today, he still hadn't texted. She knew he said that the day started tomorrow, but certainly he would let her know something today?

Kelly always hoped for the best, but she prepared for the worst, so tonight she was packing her bags.

She hoped that if Joshua was going to do something, he knew he only had tomorrow before she caught a flight back to the city.

Fifteen

"Thank you for meeting with us, Mr. Case," Sarah Findel of the school board said, sitting across from him at the round table that held two other board members.

It was odd that Joshua had lived in Sweet Blooms all his life and had worked for the school system in one fashion or another but had never seen the members of the school board. They didn't have an office in Sweet Blooms, but they did rent space in the courthouse and sometimes in the community center. He could even recall the signs that announced them coming, but he had never gone. The help he needed had been there all along.

"It was no problem, and please, call me Joshua."

"We were very excited when you contacted us," Georgia said. Georgia sat on his left.

Sarah cautioned Georgia. "Your plan on using the tree has been tried in different ways, but we haven't been able to achieve the success you've had. Any help you could give us would be great," she said, then she pointed to the woman on his right. "Roberta works in the community finding runaways and providing a safe place for teens in transition."

Roberta held out her hand. "I wanted to personally

thank you for the program you have. One of my kids who was having some problems adjusting spoke highly of you. She said you made them feel safe. In the battle for our kids, it's nice to physically know others doing the same work."

Joshua nodded at her, completely understanding her sentiments about working with someone you could actually see.

Yesterday he had discovered that it wasn't too late and he still had a chance with Kelly. He'd ask for a day, and he wanted to be able to tell her he had done everything he could to get himself help, and to let go of things that weren't healthy for him.

"Joshua," Ms. Findel said. "We've been looking at your program for some time, so it's good that you came to us with the partnership."

She gave out a copy of the grant they had written. Joshua was a little confused until he opened it up. Inside was a list of other places in Sweet Blooms, mainly businesses that wanted to be safe places for troubled teens if anything should happen to their phone.

"As you can see, there are a lot of businesses that also share your concern for the children. We have just started playing with the idea of having safe places for children to go to throughout the town. In case a teen loses their phone, or for some reason they feel as though they can't use their phone, then the businesses in this folder have agreed to offer a safe space for the teen."

Joshua looked at the list of businesses in the folder. It was more people than he expected to be interested in helping him. "I want to say thank you. I didn't know there was so much support for this subject when I first started it."

"Mr. Case, the message we want to send out is that we care about our kids. We also want everyone to be able to play a part in making sure our children are safe."

"When you have time, what I would really like to do is to make a map of all of the businesses that have agreed to help us," Roberta said. "That way we can see if we have any holes in the network."

Joshua smiled. "That would be great."

"If there is anything we can do, please let us know," Sarah Findel said.

Joshua heard what Ms. Findel said, but what he was really wanted to know was if any of them could give him some advice or at least look over his plan for Kelly tonight. He was still apprehensive about not being in control of the emergency tree, but he was confident that with training, these were the right people who should be taking the project to the next level.

He shook hands with the ladies and then left in order to prepare for tonight. As he was walking to his truck, he was checking off all the things he had to do to get ready. Now he knew he wasn't alone when it came to watching out for the teens in the town. The only thing he needed to work on now was making sure the only woman he'd ever loved didn't leave him behind.

The day had passed, and there was no sign of Joshua. Kelly had been jumpy all day long, waiting. What made it worse was the students had been waiting too. When the bell rang at the end of the day, a couple of the boys came to her and told her Mr. Case hadn't been in all day.

She knew they meant well. Kelly felt twice as stupid, though. She had come in today with her hair done, and she had worn the most impractical dress to teach in. It was a tan sundress that she knew picked up the highlights from her hair. Even the shoes had been hopeful. She had on brown wedge sandals that had a cute little strap that went over the bridge of her foot. On the strap was embroidered flowers.

She thought it was her just reward when her feet started to hurt her at the end of the day. She didn't want to name it, but as she sat in her car, she had to. Today, Kelly felt bereft and hopeless. If two people who were meant to be together couldn't get it together, what hope was there?

She had strapped the seat belt across her chest, leaned her head against the seat, and let the tears fall. There were no sounds to her tears; the howls of despair and loss would come later. This was just the precursor to the abyss of loneliness and regret that was waiting for her at the house.

She wiped her eyes and took a deep breath. She just needed to get to the cottage. Her plane ticket was already purchased, and her bags were ready. She didn't like goodbyes, and she thought about changing her flight and leaving tonight. She might not be able to find a first class ticket, but tonight she didn't want anyone trying to pay that much attention to her anyway.

Resolved to leave tonight, she pulled up in front of her home and saw what looked like Davy standing in a suit. When she parked and stepped out of the car, she gave him a look.

Immediately, Davy put up his hands.

"I just want to say that I am so glad you finally showed up!"

"Davy, what are you doing?"

Davy sighed and shook his head. "I have to tell you, Ms. Kelly, I'm not really sure. Mr. Case told me to stand here and wait for you. He also said when you get here, I'm supposed to show you to your door. That just makes no sense at all. Like you don't know where it is."

Kelly did her very best not to laugh. "And where is Mr. Case right now, Davy?"

"He's inside prepping. Oh yeah, I almost forgot." He reached into his side pocket and took out a button.

"What's that?"

Davy smiled. "It's a button to let Mr. Case know that you are here."

Kelly came around the car and held her hand out. "May I?"

"Sure! I need to go home. Unless you need help getting to the door?"

Kelly kept her mouth closed and shook her head no.

"Great! Tell Mr. Case thanks!"

Kelly watched Davy walk down the block. She could barely keep her excitement to herself. He hadn't forgotten. He had still played it to the very last minute!

Kelly couldn't get a grip on her feelings. On the one hand, she wanted to fall to the ground and cry. She was so happy that he recognized what they had and was willing to fight. But she had to admit there was a part of her that was still scared. Scared that this was just a temporary scramble and that in the future, he'd change.

Kelly remembered what her foster mom would say. *You can't make decisions based on things that haven't happened yet. If you live in tomorrow, you'll miss today.*

Tossing the button up in the air, she walked right up to her door. Then she pushed the button. Inside she heard thumps as if someone was running through the house. Then she heard a grunt that sounded like it came from Joshua. Two more steps, and then she heard what sounded like a fall and him yelling, "You've got to be kidding me."

Finally, she saw the handle on her door turn, and the door opened.

When it did, she was accosted by the smell of flowers and pasta. Joshua was dressed in a black suit, and his hair was oddly flat. She must have been looking at it a little too long because he self consciously ran his hand over his hair.

"It's okay if you don't like it. It will grow out. The girls in the teams said it was the latest style."

"Ah," she said, looking at him and knowing that this was him making an effort. He was out of his comfort zone, uncomfortable, and yet he was still here.

He looked at her and whistled, "You look amazing, and you didn't even know about everything that's going on in the house," he said.

Kelly cleared her throat. "Do you think I could come into the house?"

Then it dawned on him that he was leaning in the doorway and still hadn't let her in. "Oh. Oh, I'm so sorry. Please come in."

At first, she thought the light had blown, or that there was a 40-watt bulb in the lamp. Her place was so dark. As her eyes adjusted, she realized the reason it was so dark was that the house was only lit by candlelight. Of course, a lot of the candles were melted past their middles, and the wax on several candles had overflowed from their holders, making wax pools on the wood.

Joshua reached out and touched her shoulder. She looked in the general direction and saw him pointing upwards. Behind him was a sign that had five stars on it. She smiled and looked at Joshua.

"I know you said you wanted to go to a five-star restaurant. I looked at some of the menus, and I think I need to save up a bit for that. On top of that, I couldn't recognize a single dish on the menus. And it seems that they are really cheap. I mean, with all the money they are charging, they only give you one sheet of paper for the whole menu!"

Kelly looked away and laughed into her hand. Then a color caught her eye. It was red. When she looked closer, she could see someone had sprinkled rose petals on the floor. She looked up at Joshua.

"I think you should walk on rose petals, no matter where you go."

Kelly smiled, and then Joshua grabbed her upper arm. "Now we want to walk very slowly but firmly to the table. While the petals are pretty, I've discovered that when the petals get wilted, they can be a bit slippery."

Kelly recalled hearing the thump on the other side of the door, and now it was all clear. Finally, she was sitting at the table when she realized all of the living room furniture was gone. The table had been brought into the living room for this occasion.

Joshua disappeared and then brought out a couple of platters. He took a seat at the table and then removed the covers. It was one plate of pasta, and the other plate held a bowl with meatball sauce and meatballs in it.

That was the last straw for Kelly. She just burst out laughing. Joshua, on the other hand, had already started to explain.

"You may not know this, but my culinary skills are limited. I mean, I eat steak about every night. Steak and rice, steak and salad, or a steak sandwich. Anyway, we agreed that steak would not be the most romantic thing to serve. We tried to cook several things that just didn't survive. In the end, we picked something that we thought would be the most authentic thing to do.

"Why don't I serve the meal, and then we can get to the good part."

Kelly raised her eyebrow. Then Joshua took his fork and dug into the pasta, and there was the distinctive squish of metal against the gelatinous matter. As soon as he heard it, he shook his head. "I'll be right back. I just need to—"

Kelly reached out to him and stopped him.

"Joshua, I've seen enough."

Joshua looked around. "I'm not done. I've got—"

"Shhh, love. I've really seen enough," she said with a smile.

He looked a bit dejected. "I wanted this to be right for you, Kelly. I wanted you to know that I've shed most of my guilty habits. That I've made an appointment to talk about Jordan. That I'm working on being a better me. So I can be a better person for you."

Kelly reached out and caressed his cheek. "Joshua, I care for you just the way you are. I need you to care for me just the way I am, and to be willing to listen to me."

Joshua moved closer and leaned his forehead against hers. "I know how important communication is.

These last weeks have been pounding that into my head. Kelly, please stay. I want to try with you."

"Joshua, I'm not easy."

Joshua smiled. "Neither am I. But will you stay, anyway?"

"Oh yes, I'll stay"

Joshua stood up and held out his hand. Kelly put hers in his, and he pulled her into his embrace.

"Thank you for taking the chance," Joshua said.

"It's about trust, right?"

"Yeah, it is," he said as he lowered his head to kiss her. She wrapped her arms around his neck. Then she closed her eyes until she felt the gentle brush of his lips on hers. Kelly relaxed into him and pulled him deeper into the kiss.

When they separated, she could see the laughter in his eyes.

"You're never going to do what's expected, are you?"

Kelly looked shocked. "I'm sorry you were taking so long. I thought you needed some instructions. You do know I'm one of the best instructors you can find on the east coast."

"So I've been told. Ms. Instructor, would you be interested in dancing with me on the back lawn?"

Kelly nodded. "Yes, Mr. Case, I'd be very interested."

Both of them took off their shoes to safely make it across the floor and then went to the backyard to dance as the sun set to music he decided to hum.

Epilogue

Evan Sparrow didn't like parties. He didn't like being around a lot of people, and he really didn't like being in confined spaces. The only reason he was putting himself through this discomfort was flowing through the room like a breath of fresh air. Her name was Cassandra Olsen.

He had been intrigued with her since the first time he had met her. She had long black hair that danced when she had it down. He'd seen it in a ponytail, and even then it bounced with the energy and life she brought to everything.

Besides being beautiful, she was smart. He had heard someone say she used to be an accountant. He had come into town and seen her during the fair. She had been a backup server in the Banter House. He knew then she was the one.

Evan Sparrow was the only surviving child of the Sparrows who lived on the outskirts of town. Both of his parents had been illiterate and, as a result, had only been small farmers. When they discovered their son had a woodcutting talent, they let him make figures instead of working on the farm.

His mother had told him one day he would find a woman who looked like his art. She'd be soul beautiful, kind, and full of life. For a very long time, Evan had stopped believing that a person would ever come. Then he'd come into town to deliver his goods, and he had met her. From that moment on, he thought of little else except how to get Cassandra Olsen to realize he was a man interested in her.

He thought he had it all figured out a couple of months ago. He'd invited her out to a crafter party. He'd introduced her to everyone personally so she would know how important she was, and then, in front of everyone, he gave her an engagement bracelet.

She'd accepted it in front of the crafters and cried because she said she loved it. He was sure they were on the same page. All he had to do was prove he was ready to have a wife. It took a while and some negotiations with Robert Parker, who was running the guild for them, but he was ready. He would have a home, income, and a place for Cassandra to have her own home.

Evan thought it was a done deal until he saw her tonight and noticed she didn't have the bracelet on. The other crafters noticed too.

His friend Tom came to sit by him.

Evan held up his hand. "You don't have to tell me you told me so."

"I'm not going to."

"Good."

"I'm going to ask you a question that I don't think you thought about."

Evan looked at his friend. "Okay, go for it."

"Did you consider that she didn't know it was an engagement bracelet?"

Evan looked confused. His friend leaned closer. "Evan, I don't think she knows you two are engaged."

I hope you've enjoyed Kelly and Joshua's story. Check out Book five in the Love Happens Series *Sweet Engagement* and read about Evan and Cassandra's story.

Sign up to my newsletter to receive updates on new releases, sale promotions, and free books.

susanwarnerauthor.com